SANTA MARIA PUBLIC LIBRARY
D0481362

01
02
03

WHISTLING GIRL

WHISTLING GIRL

A Victorian Romance

ARDELL L. D. TAYLOR

Five Star
Unity, Maine

Five Star First Edition Romance Series.

First Edition, Second Printing.

Published in 2000 in conjunction with Ardell L. D. Taylor

Photography by Johnny D. Boggs

Set in 11 pt. Plantin by Anne Bradeen.

Printed in the United States on permanent paper.

Library of Congress Cataloging-in-Publication Data

Taylor, Ardell L. D. (Ardell Loretta Durrell)
Whistling girl / by Ardell L.D. Taylor.
p. cm.—(Five Star first edition romance series)
ISBN 0-7862-2854-7 (hc : alk. paper)
1. California—Fiction. I. Title. II. Series.
PS3570.A92712 W48 2000
813′.6—dc21 00-061027

To Janey, who died too soon

CHAPTER ONE

"*¡Santa Madre!*, Anita, where have you been? I hope you have not been down into the town looking like that!"

The words were in Spanish, but the reply came in English.

"No, Mamá. I have only been walking in the *chaparral.*"

"Thank the good Lord for that! You look positively indecent."

"Indecent!"

"Yes, María Anita, positively indecent. Your bosom actually quivers when you walk. Any man seeing you would think you were a loose woman. I have told you time after time to wear your corset, but you pay no attention to me."

Doña Guadalupe Aldon heaved a great sigh and her mouth took on a slight pout, a more and more frequent occurrence these days. Her speech to her daughter was mostly in the language of her youth, with an occasional English word or phrase thrown in. When she did use English, it was clear enough, spoken with a charming accent and an odd wording. To Anita, both languages came with equal ease and her responses were divided evenly between the two.

"I just don't understand," Doña Guadalupe went on, "why it should be, after giving birth to seven other children, and losing four of them, that God should give me a disobedient child like you in my old age."

"Mamá!" protested Anita. "I am not a child and I am not disobedient. I am eighteen years old and I *do* wear that . . . that miserable corset whenever I go out where I will be seen. And besides," she added designedly, knowing her mother's weaknesses, "you are not anywhere near old age. You will not be old for a long time yet."

Her mother softened at once. She was a handsome woman, vain of her creamy olive skin, still smooth and unwrinkled. After fifty-six years she retained more than a little of the beauty of her youth, which had been famous in the California of her day.

"Well, I *feel* old anyway since Alexander died. It is very hard to be a poor widow with an unmarried daughter and no money. How you will ever find a husband of your own class when we are so poor, I do not know."

It was Anita's turn to sigh. An attractive girl in her own right, she bore little resemblance to her mother. The deep dimple in her left cheek and her fair skin, turned golden by the California sun, were from her English father, Alexander Aldon. Even her dark eyes and hair were more like those of the Aldons than the Falcóns, her mother's family. Only her full, mature figure came from her mother, and it had been the cause of all her mother's worry about eligible husbands since Anita reached the age of fourteen.

To Anita, it seemed that any talk of her "own class" was foolish since the loss of their money had placed them in quite a different class but she knew better than to say so. She knew, almost word for word, the lecture she would receive about the excellence of her English ancestors, the Aldons, and the nobility of her Spanish ancestors, the Falcóns, and how the mere loss of money did not mean they had lost any of the innate refinement of those old families. It was merely that their financial straits made it more difficult for a marriageable daughter to find a suitable husband. It was an old, old complaint, one Anita had heard many times since her father's death four years ago.

Don Alejandro, as he was called, had been owner of the Rancho Las Tunas, *patrón* of many thousands of acres, hundreds of Spanish and Indian workers, and countless cattle and horses. The *rancho* had been a little kingdom of its own, like many others in California. When Don Alejandro had married the beautiful Guadalupe Falcón, he had installed his young bride as mistress of the great sprawling adobe house on its own hill at the foot of the San Gabriel mountains. She had reigned like a queen in the big house, and eight children had been born there, though only four survived. The others had been laid to rest, one by one, in the *rancho* cemetery, including the only son, long awaited and greatly mourned, who had lived a mere three years.

But all that was before the squatters had come and begun the steady, merciless stealing of land, cattle, and water. This never-ending thievery had cost Don Alejandro so much in legal fees, in a losing battle for his rights, that in the end almost all the land had been sold to pay his debts. Of all his broad acres he had managed to keep only eighty of the choicest in the foothills, his orchards, and a vineyard. All the rest, including the old house, had been lost.

Anita was not yet twelve years old when they had moved out of their old home on the hill and into the house of their former *mayordomo*. She would never forget that day. They had brought all the beautiful old furniture, many heirlooms from her mother's family, and had tried to fit it into these four little rooms. Even when the house was so crowded they could hardly move, many pieces were still outside . . . and that night it rained. She still remembered her mother sobbing over the ruin of Grandmother Falcón's hand carved chest and beautiful French dressing table.

Only a little more than two years later Alexander Aldon died, a broken man. Since then, Doña Guadalupe, his much younger wife, and María Anita, the child of his old age, had lived in the little house on the last of their property and tried to make ends meet.

For Anita it was not hard. She had loved the old home, but mostly she loved the land, as her father had. Also like her father, she loved to see what the land would grow, and it was at her instigation that a garden was planted to supply the kitchen. There were many things in her garden that were unfamiliar to most Californians of her time because Anita remembered her father's talk about the gardens he had known in his native England and in the other places he had visited before marrying and settling down in California in his middle years.

He had planted vineyards of French grapes, orchards of olives, and was one of the first to grow the new navel oranges after they were imported in '73. The vineyards and orchards were sadly in need of care, but Anita made sure that they were at least irrigated periodically.

Anita's mother took no interest in the orchards or garden and found her widowhood a great burden to her. Her one desire was to get away from the place of her mortification and she made frequent visits to her relatives in Los Angeles, never understanding why Anita had no great desire to accompany her. Doña Guadalupe was always ready to seize any excuse for one of these visits. During the years since her husband's death she had never ceased lamenting that their limited means would not allow them to move into town permanently.

"If only we could sell the last of this accursed land," she would say, "we could afford to buy a nice little house in Los Angeles and you could go to all the parties and meet all the well-to-do young men and find a nice husband."

Anita no longer made any reply to this frequently repeated remark. She had known for a long time that their savings were dwindling and that if a buyer could be found they would have to sell their remaining land just to keep living.

Doña Guadalupe had no head for figures, and a life of luxury had not prepared her for the necessity of careful spending. After the first disastrous year of her widowhood it became apparent that she could not handle her own finances, so they had been taken over by her brother, Don Jorge Falcón. Don Jorge was the oldest living male member of the family. Doña Guadalupe had been obeying one or another masculine relative all her life, so it was with great relief that she had turned over her affairs to Don Jorge. This willingness, however, did not prevent her from making constant complaints about the smallness of the monthly sum he allowed her for living expenses.

"But it is so little!" she wailed repeatedly. "Of course I have confidence in Jorge. I am sure he knows what is best. But how can we exist on so little?"

Actually, they existed quite well. Anita took over the buying of household provisions, and since her kitchen garden saved a great deal of food money, and her careful purchases saved even more, her mother was able to spend small sums for many little luxuries they could not otherwise have afforded. But Doña Guadalupe never understood this and spoke constantly of their poverty and the necessity of selling their property.

She was speaking of it now.

"It would be so much easier to meet men of your class if we could sell this place and move to Los Angeles. We are too far away from everything out here. We never see anyone."

"Oh, Mamá, Aunt Alma and Uncle Jim were here just last

week, and Don Jorge comes almost every month."

"Well, of course, the family comes. I mean other people—friends of the family and young people of your age."

"We saw lots of people at Christmastime," Anita reminded her, "and at Easter. And San Juan's Day is almost here. You know we always see everyone at Luisa's house on San Juan's Day."

Anita's oldest sister, Luisa, lived in Los Angeles with her husband and family, and it had been her custom for years to entertain the entire family, as well as some friends, on the Día de San Juan, June twenty-fourth.

Doña Guadalupe brightened. "That is true!" she exclaimed. "San Juan's Day is coming! What day is today? Run and look at your calendar."

Anita went into her bedroom where a calendar hung on the door. It seemed only a few weeks ago that her uncle Jim Taylor had given her the calendar because she had admired the pretty picture on it. It was a painting of snow-covered mountains reflected in a blue lake with strange little high-peaked houses along the shore. Under the picture was printed, in heavy black letters, FARMERS AND MERCHANTS BANK OF LOS ANGELES - 1887. Her uncle had said, "It's a new idea of Mr. Hellman's to advertise his bank. Take it if you like it." That was last Christmas, and here it was June already and the year half over.

"It is the sixteenth," she called to her mother.

"The sixteenth! Why, Día de San Juan is only a week away! Why didn't I think sooner? Luisa will need help getting everything ready. We must go in and help her."

"She won't need help so soon, Mamá," protested Anita. "She has been having the San Juan's Day party for years. She knows just how to plan everything so it is no trouble."

"Nonsense," said Doña Guadalupe. "Of course she will be

glad to have her own mother and sister there. We can pack up a few things and get Emeterio to drive us in on Sunday."

Anita sighed. She knew that nothing she could say would have any effect. Once again her mother had found an excuse to leave Las Tunas and spend a week in Los Angeles.

"All right, Mamá," she agreed, "you go. But I am not going."

"Not going? Of course you must go."

"No," she replied quietly. "I do not want to leave so soon. There is a lot of work to do in the garden, and the orange grove needs irrigating."

"María Anita, you exasperate me! Here you have a chance to go where you might meet some young men, and you prefer to stay home and work in that garden! I wish you would leave the gardening to Emeterio. How many times do I have to tell you that you will spoil your complexion working outside? Weeding and irrigating like a *peón*! A daughter of Don Alejandro Aldon and a granddaughter of Don Luis Falcón y Figueroa! *¡Dios Mío!* That I should live to see this day!"

"I *like* to work outside, especially in the garden," said Anita. "Besides, we need the vegetables."

"Vegetables!" cried Doña Guadalupe. "What we need is for you to learn to behave like a lady so that some nice young man will want to marry you! No decent young men will look at you if your skin is all brown from the sun and your hands are rough from working in the dirt."

"If that is the case, then I will not marry," said Anita firmly.

Doña Guadalupe wrung her hands.

"*¡Santa Madre!*" she cried. "And how do you think you will live if you do not marry?"

"I will go to work."

"Go to work? Doing what, in the name of God?"

"I could become a teacher," answered Anita, "or a seamstress like the station agent's wife."

"Oh, Anita, how foolish you are! You do not know what you are talking about. You could not possibly live on what you would earn that way."

"Maybe you could not," said Anita, "but I could."

Doña Guadalupe pulled a handkerchief from the bosom of her basque, put it to her eyes, and began to weep.

At once, remorse swept Anita. "Oh, don't cry, Mamá! Please do not. I am sorry that I worried you." She put a hand on her mother's arm and kissed her cheek. "*You* go and help Luisa. She will be glad to have you. But if I go, I will only be in the way. And I would really much rather stay at home. You go without me. Please."

"Well . . . will you promise not to work all day in the sun?"

"All right, Mamá. I promise."

"And you will come in later?"

"Yes, of course. I will be there for the party."

Sunday morning Anita assisted her mother with her preparations, and helped load her belongings in the wagon. Emeterio Hernandez, the old servant who lived with his wife, Concha, in a one-room house on the Aldon property, drove the wagon out to the road. Anita waved good-bye and then turned back into the house with a relief she could not deny.

She loved and pitied her mother because she understood her. Doña Gaudalupe's character was shallow and as clear as water. She had a sweet, trusting nature and had loved and been loved by everyone all her life. She believed without question whatever she was told by those who represented authority in her life—parents, husband, priests—and she had sailed serenely through life, secure in her ignorance, trusting to those others to clear every obstacle from her path. Then her safe little world had fallen apart. She had not the capacity to understand what had happened, and could only rail at fate in her helplessness, clinging to all the old dogma of her youth like a drowning person clutching at flotsam. Her daughter pitied her . . . and was glad to see her go.

Anita went back into her own room and sat down. She had been wanting to sort out her thoughts ever since her mother had questioned her so insistently about her future, but she had to be alone to think seriously; and she had deliberately postponed the effort until her mother had left. Now, as she sat down on the white counterpane of her bed, she realized that the room was stuffy and dark. She wanted to be out in the open, under the sky, with a breeze in her face.

For one wistful moment she let herself think how nice it would be to ride a horse once more as she used to do before the *rancho* was lost. How she had loved to urge her horse to a gallop and make her own breeze on hot days! She had had her own little mare, and they had roamed all over the *rancho* together. Amistosa was her name. Was it possible she was still alive . . . somewhere . . . after all these years? But those days were long over. The only horse they could afford now was the tired old animal who pulled Emeterio's wagon. Anita took herself firmly in hand. After all, she liked to walk almost as much as she had liked to ride.

She went back out into the kitchen, where Concha, the old cook, was cutting up a chicken to prepare for Sunday dinner.

"I am going for a walk, Concha," she said. "I will be back by lunchtime."

"*Bien, mi hijita.* It is too nice to stay indoors."

Anita smiled affectionately and patted the old woman's shoulder as she passed. She had always been *mi hijita,* my little daughter, to this woman who had had only sons, now long grown and departed. It was like having two mothers.

Outside, Anita took a deep breath and looked around. The summer heat had not yet begun and the day was warm and pleasant. Anita went out of the yard into the orange grove, and down an aisle between the rows of big dark trees, walking beside the old furrows long since grown over with mustard, mallow, and other weeds. On the far side of the grove she emerged into a section of *chaparral* which had never been put under cultivation and here she struck out in an apparently aimless direction, weaving her way around the bushes. After perhaps a quarter of a mile, she came to a well-worn path and turned onto it, heading toward a ridge which stretched out into the valley from the foothills ahead of her.

She walked slowly and pensively, and though her eyes took in the beauty of the mountains and of the wildflowers blooming here and there, it did not give her as much pleasure as usual. She had been depressed by the disagreement with her mother, though she was long used to similar scenes and not usually disturbed by them. But this time had been different. Her mother's desperate questions had suddenly made her aware that she really did not know how she was going to cope with the future, and if her mother's plans did not suit her, she must make some of her own.

So she followed the path to the base of the ridge and up the side to the top, where she found a grassy spot in front of a boulder and sat down. Here she leaned back against the rock and stared out over the stretch of the valley she had just crossed, to the orchard beyond, and the roofs of some of the buildings in Las Tunas beyond that. It was her home, and she loved it, but she knew that she would not be able to stay here much longer—probably not more than a year or two more at most. Property was beginning to be sold all around them, and it was only a question of time before a buyer would be found for the Aldon land.

If only they could make a living from the place! Then it would not have to be sold. Her father had believed it could be done, but he had been too old and sick those last two years before he died. Afterward, she had suggested to her uncle, Don Jorge, that something should be done with the oranges, the grapes, and the olives, but Don Jorge was a cattleman and regarded orchards and vineyards much as Anita regarded her kitchen garden—a nice addition to the household diet, but hardly a source of income.

Then she had spoken to her uncle, Jim Taylor. He was an American and he agreed with Anita that there might be some money to be made—if she could find a man who understood pruning and fertilizing and spraying and all the other necessary procedures. But Uncle Jim was a merchant, not a farmer, and he did not have the needed knowledge. Neither did Anita, though she almost thought if she could get a little money to hire a few skilled workers, her rudimentary expertise might be enough. But who was going to believe that a mere girl would know anything about such work? Certainly no one was going to give her money to experiment.

So the property would have to be sold, and they would move to Los Angeles and live on a lot, and she would never again roam the *chaparral* and climb the foothills. And how were they going to live when that money ran out? Of course, she knew the family would not let them starve, but in that respect she was in perfect agreement with her mother. She had no desire to be supported by her relatives.

She did not even consider the idea of marriage, which loomed so large in Doña Guadalupe's mind. She had never met a man she could love, and she certainly would not marry for money. She had told her mother she would become a teacher or a seamstress. She had said it without thought, simply as a defense, but now she gave it serious consideration.

She had to admit she would never make a good dressmaker; her sewing was not that good. She disliked making her own clothes and had actually paid to have her newest dress made for her by a seamstress who had recently arrived in Las Tunas.

So that left teaching. Well, it was a definite possibility. If they moved into Los Angeles she could attend the normal school that had opened a few years ago. She thought she might be a pretty fair teacher. She liked children, and her little nieces and nephews adored her. And there were plenty of places for teachers in Los Angeles. Yes, she could really do that. She might even be able to teach in the Las Tunas school. Of course! Why hadn't she thought of that? There were only three teachers there, but they changed frequently. Her spirits began to revive.

Then it occurred to her that even if they did not move to Los Angeles, she could still attend normal school by staying with Uncle Jim and Aunt Alma at their house in town. If she did that, and if she got a job soon enough, they might not even have to sell the property! She could start when the fall term began!

She laughed aloud and stood up. The weight of doubt lifted and her spirits rose to their usual level. Brushing her skirt with her hands, she wondered why she had been so downcast. There wasn't really any problem. Swiftly she descended the trail, headed for home, but as soon as she reached level ground she slowed to a saunter and began whistling "La Golondrina", feeling contented in spite of the plaintive sound of the tune.

CHAPTER TWO

It was the nineteenth of June when John Claremont Vanderburg, youngest son of W. Stuyvesant Vanderburg, the New York financier, looked out the window of the smoking car on the slowly moving train and realized that the desert he had been seeing for so many miles was at last giving way to something else.

The train had entered a rough break in the mountains and was now descending from the high desert to an altogether different landscape. Now, though he still spotted an occasional cactus, he also began to see cultivated fields and could hardly believe his eyes. Then he saw farmhouses surrounded by trees. And these trees were not the cottonwoods he had grown used to seeing at every desert oasis where the train stopped but others that were unfamiliar to him. One was large, gnarled, and spreading with dark foliage; it seemed native to the place, for he also saw that it was growing wild in some of the canyons. Another type of tree, which he often saw close to the houses, was lacy with bright green drooping branches; it resembled a willow but was not.

When the train passed close enough for him to identify the plants growing in the fields, he began looking with interest at the varied crops he saw. This was what he had come for, after all. But nothing in his previous reading or his training at the

Massachusetts Agricultural College prepared him for his shock of disbelief when he saw the first orange grove growing next to a stand of wheat as flourishing as any he had seen in the east. There were even a few oranges on the trees although he knew from his reading that it was not their principal producing season.

The train pulled into a little town, evidently the center of the farming community, and stopped. The name on the depot was San Bernardino.

What a mouthful, he thought as he attempted to repeat the name under his breath.

Several people were waiting to board the train at the station. Some appeared to be farmers obviously wearing their best clothes. One was an elderly man, very tall and straight, dressed in an outlandish costume of black material trimmed with silver pieces. He also wore a broad, flat-brimmed hat and was smoking a long, thin cigar, but none of the others on the platform seemed to pay any attention to his peculiar attire. Two ladies, apparently a mother and daughter, were accompanied by a man in an ordinary business suit. The ladies seemed quite fashionable to John, although he was aware that his sister-in-law, Alice, always laughed at him whenever he made any remark about fashions. He would have liked very much to hear her comments on these people, especially that tall, Spanish-looking fellow.

Alice was Mrs. Gordon Lawrence Vanderburg, wife of his oldest brother, and John had a great deal of respect for her opinions regarding dress, manners, and social form. She was a leader of the younger set of New York society and an exponent of the very latest modes. Even John's mother, who rarely took a backseat to anyone, admitted that Alice was an expert in the matter of fashion.

"Look what she's done for Gordon," his mother had said

to him. "Since they've been married, he's become the best-dressed man in New York, and you could be the same if you'd just ask Alice's advice before you bought your clothes."

"I suppose that's a polite way of telling me you don't like the way I dress," said John, who had heard similar complaints before.

"Well, dear," replied his mother, "you know you've always been careless about your wearing apparel; and I did overhear Mrs. Astor telling Miss Stanford that she didn't see how a brother of Gordon Vanderburg could be so *démodé*. At least," she added, "I think you should have some new things made before we go to Newport this year."

So he had taken his mother's advice and consulted his sister-in-law, who had very kindly accompanied him to a tailor shop and one or two haberdasheries. The result was eminently pleasing to everybody. John had had the satisfaction of knowing that he cut a very fine figure on the lawns and in the ballrooms of Newport that season. Even he could see that the year's crop of debutantes cast many a languishing glance at him over their croquet mallets and their dance programmes.

Even Miss Millicent Carrington had looked kindly on him that year, and she the Beauty of the season. He had paid his court to her all the following winter and left his cards at her door and sent his flowers with the other dozen young men who did the same. But she had accepted young Mr. Winslow of Winslow, Smythe and Winslow, and though John had murmured suitably regretful remarks and done his best to appear properly woebegone, he was conscious that his regret was merely good form.

That was the same year he had tried, and failed, to become interested in his father's business. Installed in his own small room in Vanderburg and Sons' fashionable office, he had struggled manfully to learn the ins and outs of the Stock Exchange and the Board of Trade under the guidance of his father and both older brothers. He had only become bored. In fact, his "romance" with Miss Carrington was a direct result of his boredom. She was a refreshing change from stocks and bonds, and she waltzed beautifully.

It was after she accepted young Winslow that John decided he could no longer face the Stock Exchange. He confronted his father in the library one evening after dinner.

"Father," he began, "I'm afraid I'm not much of an asset to the Vanderburg offices. I'm sorry."

His father smiled. "Well, son," he said kindly, "we don't all pick up things as quickly as others. Keep working, and I'm sure you'll fit in eventually."

"I'm sure I would, but I'm not sure I want to," John replied ruefully. "I've been thinking I'd like to go back to college. After all," he hurried on as he saw his father's raised eyebrows, "you have Gordon and Bert both in the business; you don't really need me."

"Yes, of course, Gordon has a good head and takes a great deal off my shoulders, and Bert's doing very well, but there's always room for one more, and we've always expected you'd join us."

His father puffed on his cigar and looked speculatively at his son. "What did you have in mind to study if you go back to Harvard? I hope you're not thinking of more philosophy and Greek. I never could see the good of that sort of thing, unless you intend to become a teacher."

"No," John said with a smile, "no more liberal arts."

"I know that was your mother's idea. Culture is a fine thing, but it doesn't make money," continued the older man. "Law, now, would be good, or medicine, or possibly engineering."

"I was thinking of agriculture."

"Agriculture!" His father's eyebrows went all the way up this time, and he jerked the cigar from his mouth. "You want to be a goddamned farmer? There's no money in farming! Why, my grandfather was a farmer and nearly died in the poorhouse. He would have, too, if my father hadn't supported him at the last."

"I know, Father," John said quietly. "I've seen the old place. It was a typical upstate New York farm, a family operation aimed at self-sufficiency, growing a little bit of everything, definitely not a money maker."

"That's an understatement! Why, if the old folks saw a hundred dollars in cash from one end of the year to the next, they thought it was a lot! My mother never stopped being grateful to my father for bringing her to the city."

"I know all that," said John, "but that's exactly why I'd like to *study* agriculture. I think the old folks went at it wrong. Well, not wrong exactly. Their methods were all right for pioneer days. But I don't see why in these modern times a farm can't be run like a business, strictly for profit."

He hastened to elaborate. "I saw some farms out west when Mother and I went out to Chicago last year that made me think about it. You should see the grain fields out there, miles and miles of nothing but grain, a cash crop and nothing else. I got the idea then that I'd like to try it scientifically. This is the age of science, and I don't see why it shouldn't apply to farming as well as anything else."

He had gone on and explained his vision to his father: how he wanted to grow strictly for the market—whatever would sell well—and use only the best modern methods to produce the finest possible crops and command the highest prices. In the end he had convinced his father of his sincerity, if not his wisdom, and the following fall he had begun his studies at Amherst.

As his learning progressed, his interest had increased instead of lessening, as his father had expected, and his ideas for the future had begun to take form. On his visits home, he was so enthusiastic and so convincing in discussions with his father that the older man found himself beginning to change his opinion. By the time John got his degree, father and son had reached an agreement. John was to start his farming as a business enterprise with the full backing of Vanderburg and Sons, the company retaining a one-third interest in whatever ventures he should decide upon. The agricultural aspect of the business was to be entirely under John's direction, and he would be able to buy out the company interest at any time.

John vindicated himself from the very first. That year had been a bumper one for wheat, and because there was so much of it, prices had been low and the growers had lost money. He had traveled through upstate New York looking for farmland to rent, and he had heard farmer after farmer telling tales of losses and disappointments.

"Goin' t' plant oats next year," (or buckwheat or rye) "ain't no money in wheat."

"My neighbor down the road had his land in corn instead of wheat, and he made money. I'm goin' t' plant corn next year."

"I had fifty acres in wheat an' barely cleared my costs. I'll be glad t' rent it to ye, if ye want it. I'm goin' t' stick t' my apple orchards next year. Always make a little off'n them."

John had rented five hundred acres and with hired hands to help had planted it all in wheat. The local farmers laughed at him for a city slicker while they tilled their oats and rye. But the following year the price of wheat was high because there was very little supply to meet the demand, and John made a killing.

The next year he again correctly estimated the market and

made a tidy profit on broom corn. His father and brothers began to look at him with new respect.

"It's just like the Board of Trade," he told them. "You have to make an educated guess which commodities are going to go up and which are going down."

That autumn of 1886 he had come into the city feeling happier than ever before. He was tanned and healthy from his summer in the country and the season's debutantes made much of him. He was pleased to be admired and respected, but he found the usual teas and balls irksome, and the constant attention to the newest modes seemed sillier to him than it had before. He contrasted the fashion plates he saw in the ballrooms with the down-to-earth folk of the country, and he found the city people had sunk lower in his estimation. They used better grammar, but their interests were frivolous.

His greatest pleasure that winter was a visit to one of his former teachers at Amherst. Professor William Taylor was a middle-aged family man with mild blue eyes and a well-trimmed beard. He welcomed John into his small home and introduced him to his wife and children with genuine warmth. After a pleasant family dinner, John and his host settled down to a long talk beside the parlor fireplace. John related his recent experiences and confided his future hopes.

"Eventually," he said, "I want to buy my own land. But I can't decide where. I want too many different things. I'd like to try my hand at grapes, but I also want to be able to grow grain and try truck gardening as well. I think I'll take a look out around Illinois and Iowa."

"Have you thought of California?" asked his host.

"California!" exclaimed John. "I thought there was nothing out there but prospectors and cattle ranchers."

"Oh, they have those all right," Taylor admitted and his blue eyes twinkled, "but they have a lot more besides. I have a brother out there, been there for twenty years or so," he went on, "He headed out just on a pleasure trip when he was young and fell in love with the place. He's still in love with it, too. You should read his letters! He's always telling us how great the climate is and how beautiful the country, and how foolish we are to stay here in the cold."

"But what about the farming?" asked John. "Can they really grow things? It's not just a desert?"

"Here," replied Taylor getting up. "I have a book you can take that will tell you all about it." He went to a corner bookcase and took down a small volume. "It's called *California for Health, Pleasure and Residence* by Charles Nordhoff. He tells of meeting a farmer driving into Los Angeles in January with a load of produce including oranges, pumpkins, corn, green peas and some other things I've forgotten. You'll find it very interesting."

John *had* found it interesting. He had found it so interesting that he had gone on to read everything he could about California and concluded that he would never be satisfied until he had traveled there himself to see how much of what he had read was truth and how much was exaggeration. The winter was almost over when he reached his decision, and he wondered if he should wait until the following winter to make the trip. But one day his brother Gordon had approached him with a plan.

"Alice and I are going out to San Francisco in April. We've been invited to spend a couple of months with an old school friend of Alice's. Though between you and me," he added, "it's more business than pleasure."

"How is that?" asked John.

"Well, this friend of Alice's is one of Fenton Collingwood's daughters. You know, the railroad magnate? She's a widow and has moved back home with her old man, and now she's sent Alice this invitation. Father and Bert and I have been trying to get Collingwood to give us his business for quite a while without much luck. Now Father figures that if Alice and I go out there and actually spend time in Collingwood's home, he can hardly ignore us in a business way."

"That sounds reasonable," John said.

"Since you want to see the west coast, too, why don't you head out a few weeks after us, and we can meet somewhere after Alice and I finish buttering up old Collingwood? We can all spend some time looking around and then come home together."

So here John was at the beginning of summer, entering California on a train headed for Los Angeles. In his suitcase he carried a letter of introduction to Professor Taylor's brother. The brother's name was James Taylor, and he had a hardware business.

The rest of the journey to Los Angeles John kept moving from one side of the train to the other as he found himself fascinated by the views on either hand. The train passed through mile after mile of sparsely settled country, rolling hills and flat brushland stretching down from a sharply rising mountain range, along the base of which the train was crawling. For the most part the valley was brown and dry-looking yet oddly attractive to John's eyes. On the opposite side greenery could occasionally be seen in the mouths of canyons and along the course of the shallow streams that flowed out from those canyons. But most startling of all to John was the sudden appearance of lush green fields and orchards in the midst of the brown wilderness whenever the train passed an outlying farm or settlement.

One such place he noticed in particular because of the row

of small houses he could see close to the tracks. Each little yard was shaded by large trees and overflowing with flowers. Roses, especially, seemed almost to grow wild, so luxuriously did they cover fences and climb over porches. Obviously, where there was water here, things grew and grew well. John read the name of the place on the depot sign as they passed. It was Las Tunas.

At last, turning away from the mountains, the train rolled through a park-like grassland sprinkled with huge, gnarled trees, across a deep, dry canyon, through some rolling hills, and into the booming town of Los Angeles. He caught glimpses first of many small farms, giving way to neat residential streets, then closely-built commercial buildings, and finally, as the train came to a stop, a station, the newness of which was plain to the eye.

As he descended from the car, he was accosted by a young man, well dressed and smiling affably.

"Welcome to California, sir. I'm Bill Cameron of Cameron Land and Development Company. My card, sir. If you're looking for property, we have many fine pieces we'd be happy to show you."

John took the card."Why, thank you. Perhaps after I'm settled . . ."

"Any time, sir, any time," said the affable Mr. Cameron, and he moved on to present his card to another passenger just descending from the train.

John was still looking at the business card in his hand when a voice spoke loudly behind him.

"Just in time! Just in time, folks, for the big land auction tomorrow. Hundreds of beautiful homesites in the brand-new town of Burbank! Here's our announcement, madam, and one for you, sir," said the promoter, thrusting a sheet of paper at John. It was printed in red ink:

DON'T MISS THIS
FANTASTIC OPPORTUNITY!
Over 300 Lots in
BEAUTIFUL BURBANK
Will Be Sold At
AUCTION
12 NOON TUESDAY JUNE 20TH
NEW BURBANK CIVIC PLAZA
FREE
PICNIC LUNCH, COFFEE, & LEMONADE
COME ONE, COME ALL!

John thrust the paper into his pocket and made his way through the station building and out to the street where a line of hacks were waiting.

Since it was well after business hours by the time he had settled into his hotel and enjoyed a leisurely meal in the dining room, he decided to take a walk around town before bedtime. Accordingly, he left his hotel, the Nadeau, at First and Spring, and walked north. He noted the Acme Hardware, James Taylor's place of business, in the middle of the block below Arcadia Street, where he turned east to Main, then south again and back to the Nadeau.

He returned to his room with the impression of a raw frontier town with dusty, unpaved streets and mostly wooden sidewalks. He had seen saloons, restaurants, and real estate dealers in plenty, but only one theater.

CHAPTER THREE

The week before San Juan's Day passed quickly and pleasantly for Anita. Mindful of her promise to her mother, she had confined her gardening to the mornings, when the sun was not so hot, and sometimes an hour or two in the evening after the sun had set.

Once, she had put on her corset, a clean dress, and a hat and walked down into the small but growing settlement of Las Tunas. It was still a matter of amazement to her that a town was sprouting on ground that used to be devoted to her father's horse corrals. The present owner, Mr. Lawson, had subdivided the land and laid out streets where the mares and colts used to graze, and the two-story brick building he had erected on the corner of Las Tunas Avenue and Lawson Street stood on the very spot where a stable had sheltered Don Alejandro's prize stallion. The new brick structure housed a grocery on the ground floor, where Anita made some purchases.

As she left the store, she noticed a sign announcing that one Carter P. Clarke, D.D.M., had opened an office upstairs, where he was available for dentistry. Dr. Clarke was new to Las Tunas. The other office upstairs was occupied by a lawyer who had moved in as soon as the building was finished. Anita suspected he was a friend of Mr. Lawson's, which automatically made him a shyster in her mind.

Across the street another new building was going up, the latest in the ever-growing number of small wooden structures. She wondered what sort of business it was going to hold.

Farther along she approached Lawson's office and saw Mr. Willetts, Lawson's clerk, standing in front with a sunburned, pale-eyed man, plainly a rancher, who took off his battered hat when he saw Anita and stepped aside for her to pass before turning back to Willetts.

"Shore, I'd like to buy a grove, but I cain't afford it," he was saying. "I was hopin' you'd have somethin' t' lease . . . on shares mebbe."

"Sorry," Willetts replied. "Mr. Lawson's only interested in selling."

She had gone another half block before the idea hit her. The man wanted to lease an orange grove and pay the owner a share of his profit on the crop! Why couldn't her mother's land be leased out?

She stopped walking and stood still for a moment, strongly tempted to run back and speak to the man. The thought of her mother's disapproval stopped her. She giggled to herself as she imagined the horrified look on Doña Guadalupe's face if Anita were to tell her she had accosted a strange man on the street. "María Anita! Ladies *never* speak to a man until they have been introduced! And only loose women approach men on the public street."

Well, it did not matter. If one man wanted to lease an orange grove, others must, too. Perhaps they could advertise. She would speak to Uncle Jim about it. She was sure he would think the effort was worthwhile. Leasing the land would provide an income. Maybe not very much, but better than nothing. Of course, her mother would still want to move to

Los Angeles, and Anita would have to go along, but at least they would still own the land, and who knew what might happen in the future?

On Thursday the weather turned hot, but Anita had arranged with the *zanjero,* who was in charge of the irrigation canals, to direct the flow into the orange grove. She went out personally to open the sluice and let the water run into the old furrows. It would have been better if she could have had the grove cultivated and fresh furrows put in, but the old ones would have to do. She spent the morning with a hoe, checking the furrows to keep the water from breaking out. By afternoon Emeterio returned from his morning's job and took over the chore from her. She was glad to return to the house; it was hot work.

She spent the afternoon inside the house and did not go out into the garden until after supper. Then she enjoyed a quiet hour among her plants. Only one more day, she thought, before the Día de San Juan and the big party in town.

The thought of the party gave Anita somewhat mixed feelings. The twenty-mile drive in the wagon was always pleasant, and she enjoyed seeing her aunts and uncles and her many cousins, nieces, and nephews; but she could never get used to having the celebration at Luisa's house in Los Angeles.

All during her childhood it had been her father who entertained the family here at Rancho Las Tunas. The festivities had been held in the huge *patio* of the old adobe house where she had been born, complete with musicians and dancing and a whole steer roasted in a pit. The Día de San Juan had been celebrated all day and all night. Compared to those times, San Juan's Day at her sister's house seemed very tame and sedate.

But the memory of the past did not really make her unhappy. The past was long departed and the world was still a beautiful place. She was young, and she had a new dress to wear to the party.

The next morning Anita discovered that the raspberries in her garden were ripe, and consequently she spent a very warm hour among the brambles. The berries were thick on the vines and the picking was slow work, but she was rewarded with a heaping bowl full of the delicate fruit.

When she walked into the kitchen with them, Concha stared at her, aghast.

"Oh, señorita! Look at you. One would think you were of the common people instead of *la gente de razon!*"

Anita wiped the sweat from her nose with a berry-stained hand and frowned impatiently. "You are as bad as Mother! One cannot pick berries without soiling one's hands and clothes."

She deposited her bowl of raspberries on the heavy antique table that served for kitchen work as well as for meals and went out to the washstand under the *ramada* outside the back door.

"But you should not be picking the berries, María Anita, or digging the carrots or pulling the weeds as you do," protested the old woman, following her to stand in the doorway. "Why can you not wait for me to pick things and for Emeterio to do the digging and weeding?"

"Because you are too busy already, Concha *mía*. And it is hard for you to work in the hot sun. You know it is. And poor Emeterio," she went on as she rubbed soap over the scratches and stains on her arms, "has enough to do in Mr. Lawson's garden and at the new hotel."

"Well, that is true," conceded the maid, "but still it is not right. You should not be out in the hot sun. Look how dark you are getting! You should stay inside during the heat, and keep your skin white or the gentlemen will never look at you." After this pessimistic conclusion, old Concha went back to her work, shaking her head.

Anita smiled ruefully to herself. *I must really look a fright*, she thought, *if I have shocked Concha into calling me* señorita. *I have not been anything but* mi hijita *for a long time.*

After washing she went back through the kitchen into her own room and stood looking into the bevel-edged mirror on the front of the great mahogany wardrobe, so out of place in the tiny chamber.

"No wonder!" she said as she saw her reflection and laughed aloud. Her cheeks were flushed from her labor in the heat of the garden, her face and arms distinctly brown, her hair tangled by the briars, and even the sleeves of her basque had acquired one or two rips. "Oh, well, it is an old one and getting a little tight in the bosom."

Then she giggled.

"Of course I know what Mamá would say: 'If you would only wear your corset, María Anita, your clothes would fit properly.' Well, I will put on the corset tomorrow and look like a lady at the party, but today I will be comfortable."

She combed the snarls from her long dark hair and twisted it into a French knot at the back of her head, which gave her a dignity belied by the dimple in her left cheek when she smiled at herself in the mirror. The false air of stateliness amused her, and she began to whistle "La Golondrina" to herself as she returned to the kitchen to join Concha for the midday meal.

"Now you look like a lady, *mi hijita,*" said the old woman as she set a bowl of soup in front of Anita. "But you sound like a boy with your whistling," she added as she took a plate of warm *tortillas* from the back of the stove. "Why can you not be a lady all the time?"

"Well, to tell the truth," replied Anita honestly, "I think that ladies are very dull."

Concha threw up her hands. "*¡Qué tontería!* What foolishness! You think it dull to have handsome *caballeros* come to court you?"

"All the *caballeros* I have seen so far," said Anita, calmly tearing a *tortilla* in half, "have been very boring, and not very handsome, either. And, besides, if they do not like me as I am, what is the use of pretending? I cannot pretend forever."

"*¡Por supuesto, no!* Of course not! One has only to pretend until after the wedding. *Dios* only knows why the men have such funny ideas how women should act, but we have to humor them until after they have knelt before the priest with us and then we can let them know, *poco a poco*, how silly their notions are."

Anita looked seriously at the old woman. "But that does not seem fair to me, Concha, to make them think they are getting something they are not. It is cheating."

"Cheating! *¡Por Dios!* Do they not cheat *us* if they get a chance? Do they not swear eternal faithfulness to us and then hardly wait for the first baby to come before they are visiting the girls in the *cantinas?*"

Anita blushed, but the old woman continued. "Believe me, *hijita,* it is a hard world for women. You must look out for yourself and do whatever you have to do, but above all things, never let the men think you are not a lady."

Anita ate quietly for a while. Then she said wistfully, "Surely they are not *all* unfaithful. What about my father? And Emeterio? I do not think that Emeterio has been unfaithful to you."

"*Pues, sí,* your father was a true *caballero,* a real gentleman, and Emeterio is a good man as men go, but there have been times . . ." Concha shrugged her fat shoulders expressively.

"He is late today," said Anita after a moment.

"Yes. He was going to stop by the hotel on his way home to see if there was any work for him this afternoon. I hope he will have a few hours free; I want to send him up into the mouth of the *cañón* to get me some leaves of the *yerba santa*. I promised Juanita Ortiz I would make a tea for her little girl who has a bad throat."

"You do not need to wait for Emeterio," said Anita. "Give me a bag to put the leaves in and I will go and get them for you."

"You have been out in the sun all morning and now you talk of walking miles into the *cañón* and back?"

"It is a beautiful day and I feel like walking," insisted Anita. "I will take a hat to keep the sun off my face," she added, seeing the look Concha gave her.

"And long sleeves?"

"All right, long sleeves, too."

Only a few wisps of clouds floated in the deep blue of the sky and a mockingbird was practicing his repertoire as Anita stepped out of the house and started out to the road. She whistled a trill in answer to the mockingbird, then began "La Golondrina" again but thought better of it until she was past the big pepper trees in the yard and well down the road out of Concha's hearing. Then she puckered her red lips and let out the melody full and clear.

It was a song all Californians loved, and it was Anita's favorite. Her cousins in Los Angeles preferred the new American ballads such as "Love's Old Sweet Song," but Anita thought the Spanish one was prettier than any of them.

She had taught herself to whistle when quite a small girl

after hearing her cousin, Silverio Falcón, two years older than she, demonstrating the art. He had assured her with masculine conceit that girls couldn't do it, so of course she set out to prove him wrong and did so with satisfying thoroughness. Unfortunately, the accomplishment did not gain her the admiration she had expected. When she first demonstrated her ability to her Uncle Jim Taylor, he shook his head disapprovingly.

" 'Whistling girls and crowing hens/Always come to no good ends,' " he recited emphatically. "Pretty little ladies like you should not whistle."

She was surprised and disappointed but not convinced, until forced to it by a solid wall of familial disapproval. Her mother was horrified, her aunts shocked, and even her dear, indulgent father shook his head and said he hoped she would not spoil her pretty mouth that way.

After that she did not whistle in front of her family and only occasionally before old Concha and her husband, Emeterio, who were servants after all, though very privileged since they were all who were left of the great household of which they had once been a part. Concha had always been a shining light in the kitchen and Emeterio had been in charge of the gardens.

He still cared for those same gardens, only they belonged to Mr. Lawson instead of the Aldons, and Emeterio was paid by the day for his labor. The payment was small, and since the new hotel had been built, he had added to his income by tending the potted palms on the verandah and doing odd jobs for the manager. Between times he worked with Anita in the kitchen garden, helped irrigate the vineyard and groves, tended the horse and drove the wagon, and lent his stooped shoulders to many other tasks. It was a hard life for an old man, but he had never known any other existence and he was content.

When Anita reached the turn in the road that led down into the main part of the little town, she saw Emeterio sitting in the shade of a big eucalyptus tree, rolling a cigarette out of brown paper and tobacco from a pouch which he carried in the pocket of his sweat-stained shirt. He was a lean and leathery man with high brown cheekbones, a drooping mustache, and thick gray hair showing under the brim of his wide straw hat. His faded old eyes twinkled as he looked at her.

"Ay, *mi hijita,* walking again? You are young and never tired like me."

Anita smiled. "Oh, no, I am never tired, but I will sit with you a moment while you rest," and she gathered her skirts around her and sat down on the ground beside the him.

"On the ground, *mi hijita?*" he protested as she settled herself.

"It is not the first time," she answered and watched his worn brown fingers deftly shape his smoke. When it was rolled and lit, he spoke again.

"I suppose I have missed the meal," he said, "and the old woman will not want to build up the fire again."

"Don't worry," Anita assured him, "I think the soup will still be warm when you get there."

"I would have come sooner," said Emeterio, slowly blowing smoke from his nostrils, "but there are several guests at the hotel, and I was wanted to run errands for them."

"I suppose they are rich ladies too lazy to walk to the store for themselves," Anita said contemptuously.

"Yes," he replied, "there are some ladies, and it is as you say; they pay me to do their walking. Ladies don't like to walk very far. Except you, *mi hijita,*" he added, smiling ruefully.

"I know," said Anita, dimpling at him, "I do not act like a lady. My mother tells me that all the time and I even shocked

Concha into telling me so this morning. But never mind. The hotel ladies will not see me until I ride past in our wagon to-morrow and by that time I promise you I will be very ladylike. But of course," she added, "it will all be wasted if there are only ladies at the hotel and no men, since everyone says it is the men I am supposed to please."

Emeterio threw back his head and laughed. "You will please them, little one, never fear. And there are men at the hotel, too. There is a *pobre enfermo,* a young man here for his health. He has bad lungs, he told me, but he said he would run his own errands because he must walk and breathe the good warm air."

"Well, that is one man I need not worry about pleasing," said Anita, jumping to her feet. "I will go on now. I am going to the *cañón* to pick *yerba santa* for Juanita Ortiz's little girl. Concha was going to send you, but I felt like taking a nice long walk, so I said I would go instead. Now maybe you can take a little *siesta* in the hammock after you have your soup."

"That was a kindly thought," said Emeterio. "Enjoy yourself, then. And, *mi hijita . . .*"

"Yes?"

"If you whistle "La Golondrina" as you were doing coming down the road, I will not tell anyone," he promised and he laughed again.

After leaving Emeterio, Anita turned north away from the center of town and followed the road as it curved to the west and wound around the base of the mountain. Shortly before she reached the place where the river flowed from the canyon, she turned off the road and worked her way up the side of the hill to a spot where the bushes she was seeking grew in abundance.

It was a warm day, and she found herself perspiring freely.

She mopped her face with a handkerchief she was glad she had stuffed in a pocket in the seam of her skirt before leaving home. But before starting to fill her bag with the pungent leaves, she succumbed to temptation and rolled up the long sleeves of her basque.

"I said I would wear them; I didn't say I'd keep them down," she muttered and giggled.

When the bag was full, she sat down on a rock outcropping to look out over the valley. The river in its wide, gravelly bed wound off to the southwest. At this time of the year the water level was already beginning to drop, and the river was hardly more than a small creek by eastern standards, but Anita had never seen a larger watercourse. To her, it was *el río* and she loved to see the sun glinting on the water in the distance.

Seeing it reminded her that she was thirsty, and she determined to climb farther up the hillside to the flume that brought water from the canyon to the ditches of the town.

I will go home by the trail along the ditch, she thought. *It will be longer but nicer.*

Catching up her skirts in one hand and her bag in the other, she clambered over the rocks and through the brush until she reached the trail at the point where the flume poured its water into a ditch. Out of breath and panting, she knelt down and thrust cupped fingers into the flow, lifting handfuls to her mouth until her thirst was quenched. Then she put the bag down and using both hands, splashed the cold mountain water on her hot face.

"That's better," she sighed and got to her feet again.

She took her time, following the path beside the ditch. All Southern Californians prized flowing water because it was so scarce, and Anita also loved the mountain and the *chaparral* through which the water flowed. Wildflowers bloomed here and there among the bushes near the ditch, and on the hillside above her she caught sight of a yucca with its tall stalk holding aloft a great cluster of creamy white flowers, though it was late in the season for them. She passed a big patch of lupines and was tempted to pick a bouquet, but she knew they would wilt before she reached home.

After making many twists and turns following the curve of the foothills, the ins and outs of many small arroyos, the ditch descended onto comparatively level ground and passed through a grove of eucalyptus trees that had been planted by Don Alejandro Aldon years before with the idea that they might be used for lumber. Here the ditch widened, and the water flowed smoothly and quietly. Anita took off her hat and sat down in the shade beside the canal. She pulled up her skirts to let the air cool her legs and at once decided to take off her shoes and stockings.

I'll wash my feet, she thought. *It will make the rest of the walk home more comfortable.*

She untied the laces in her high-topped shoes and pulled them off gratefully, the long cotton stockings after them, and thrust her hot little feet into the water.

I'll just sit here a while, it feels so good, she thought. And wiggling her toes happily, she puckered up her lips and began to whistle.

CHAPTER FOUR

It was nine o'clock Tuesday morning when John again walked up Spring Street on his way to present himself to Mr. James Taylor.

He had been awakened early by the brilliant sunlight and clear blue sky outside his hotel window, but he had deliberately dawdled over his ablutions. He had dressed in what he considered a casual, almost sporty summer suit, kidskin gloves, and bowler hat. He was not aware that every finely tailored line, every correct and expensive appurtenance proclaimed his eastern origin. The waiter in the hotel dining room had taken one look at him and immediately formed a rosy expectation of large tips. John was therefore very assiduously served—and did not disappoint the expectation.

After breakfast he had purchased a newspaper, the *Times*, and a cigar and spent a comfortable hour in the lobby enjoying them both. The *Times* had a great deal to say about the current boom in real estate and also had many large advertisements extolling the beauties of homesites in various nearby locations.

By the time John stepped out into the bright morning sunlight, the streets were already dusty from early traffic, and the day was growing warm—so warm, in fact, that after he had covered several blocks up the street, the shade of the wooden awning in front of the Acme Hardware was very welcome. Even more so was the cool air of the dim interior when John stepped in through the recessed double doors. He passed displays of tools, bins of nails, and high rows of well-stocked shelves behind a counter where a dark-complexioned clerk was waiting on two roughly dressed men, equally dark and apparently farmers or ranchers.

"*¿Algo más?*" said the clerk, and John realized they were speaking in Spanish.

Toward the back another man was stacking boxes on a shelf. He turned to John with a pleasant smile under clear blue eyes.

"May I help you, sir?"

"I'm looking for Mr. Taylor."

"He's in the office," the man said, pointing to a partitioned corner at the back of the room. The door of the office stood open, and as John approached, he could see a portion of a cluttered roll-top desk and a heavy-set man leaning over a ledger. He was a middle aged man with brown hair and mustache, bearing scant resemblance to the professor, his brother.

"Good morning," said John. "I'm John Vanderburg, from New York." He removed an engraved card from his silver card case and handed it to Taylor. "I'm a former student of Professor Taylor at Amherst."

The hardware merchant laid his pen down upon the ledger in front of him and took John's card in ink-stained fingers.

"John Claremont Vanderburg," he read slowly. "Vanderburg. Related to W. Stuyvesant Vanderburg?"

"My father."

"Well! Very happy to meet you, Mr. Vanderburg," said Taylor, standing up. He laid the card on the ledger, hurriedly wiped his fingers on a blotter, and proffered his hand to John with a smile. The smile, at least, resembled the professor, though the rest of the man did not.

"I have a letter here for you from Professor Taylor," said John, reaching into an inside pocket. "It is entirely due to him that I am here. He lent me a book on California that made me very much interested in the agricultural possibilities out here."

The familiar smile broadened, and real warmth came into Taylor's eyes. He chuckled.

"Charles Nordhoff's work. I sent him that book. Bread upon the waters! Well, young man, you've come to the right place! Sit down." He motioned to a chair next to the desk and settled back in his own seat. "It's always gratifying to us Californians when we succeed in converting another poor, benighted easterner."

"Californian? But you're not . . ."

"The adopted ones are worse than the natives. My wife is a native, and she'll make you welcome, but not with the real, deep down pleasure of somebody like me, who knows the climate you come from. I still remember what it was like to wade snowbanks in the winter and slap mosquitos in the summer. My wife's never had that pleasure."

John laughed. "Well," he said, "I'm not converted yet; but I think I might be."

"You will be. This is the finest country in the world, whether you want to spend a vacation or a lifetime . . . Excuse me," he went on, "I'll just have a look at what my brother Bill has written."

He read the letter through, then folded it and looked quizzically at John. "Well. It's a little hard to believe you're the man he talks about in this letter. You don't look like a farmer."

John smiled. "Even farmers dress up when they come to town."

"Hmm. Yes. But not generally in the height of fashion."

"I like to think I represent the modern farmer," said John, "or the future farmer, if you prefer. I don't intend to scratch the dirt for a meager subsistence. I intend to make money. Farming is a business like any other business if you look at it that way. Sure, I can plow a furrow—I've done it—but if my margin of profit is so low that I can't afford to hire a plowman, I'm in the wrong business."

"And if the crops fail?"

"Diversify," said John. "I intend to farm hundreds of acres, several different types of land, and raise a variety of crops. If you have a bad year in one, the others will tide you over. That's why I've come to California. From what I've read, a greater variety of crops grow here than in any place I've ever heard of."

"That's certainly true," replied Taylor.

"I want to see those crops growing. I want to talk to some of your successful farmers. And then I may want to buy some land."

"Well! That's very interesting. We can certainly accommodate you on the first two parts of your program, and we can introduce you to any number of real estate men who can help you out on the last part.

"Let me get my partner in here. I'd like him to meet you. Steve!" he called. "Step in here, will you?"

The blue-eyed man who had spoken to John earlier appeared in the doorway. He was sandy-haired, good-looking, and appeared to be in his middle thirties.

"Steve, I'd like you to meet Mr. John Vanderburg of New York. This is my partner, Stephen Carson, Mr. Vanderburg. Mr. Vanderburg is out here to look over the country with an eye to farming. He may want to buy some land if he likes what he sees."

"Glad to meet you," said Carson as the two men shook hands.

"I thought between the two of us," Taylor went on, "we could give Mr. Vanderburg a pretty complete tour. If you'll show him around town this morning, Steve, while I finish up these damned accounts, then we can all have lunch together, and this afternoon I'll get my buggy and take him on a drive out through some of the farming areas. How's that strike you?"

"Fine with me," Carson agreed with a friendly twinkle in his blue eyes.

"I hadn't intended to take you away from your business," demurred John. "I thought you could just tell me what I ought to see and where to go to see it."

"Nonsense!" cried Taylor.

"No indeed!" Carson added. "I'll be happy to show you around. We're pretty proud of our town, you know, and it's always a pleasure to show it off to people from the east. We were easterners once ourselves."

Taylor grinned at John. "What did I tell you about making converts?"

John couldn't help smiling, too. "But your business . . ." he protested.

Carson tilted his head toward the front of the store. "Nothing that Pedro can't handle for a while. Come along. I'll pick up my coat and hat. What do you say, Jim, to lunch at the Elite?"

"Fine. I'll meet you there at twelve."

Mr. Carson had then proceeded to "show" Los Angeles to John. The tour had been partially on foot, partially by horsecar, and partially by hack and had covered the town from the center of the commercial district at Main and Arcadia to the very edge of the residential area at Sixth and Pearl where the horsecar line ended. John had seen every important place of business; he had viewed the old Spanish church on the Plaza; he had gazed over the view from the top of Bunker Hill; and he had admired the fine homes on Fort Street.

He had found it all very provincial. When Carson assured him enthusiastically that Los Angeles was soon going to rival San Francisco, John recalled the open water ditches he had seen along the residential streets as well as the cows grazing in vacant lots, and was inclined to be amused.

But Carson was serious. "They got ahead of us up there because of the gold discovery," Steve Carson said, "but we have the better climate, and it's inevitable that we'll catch up once easterners realize what we've got here. And they *are* realizing it!" he exclaimed. "The real estate business is booming. The old *ranchos* are being broken up, the land subdivided, and new towns are starting up all around us, with Los Angeles right in the center of everything.

"I've been here six years myself," he went on, "and the changes I've seen in that time are amazing."

"Where are you from, then?" asked John.

"Cincinnati," replied Steve Carson. "My folks had a small hardware business back there where I worked as a kid. I came out here out of curiosity, just to see the country. Then, when my dad died, I sold everything back there and came out here for good.

"I went to work for Jim first thing, and we hit it off right from the start. He's been like a second father to me, really. When I found out he wanted to expand the business and didn't have the money, I offered him mine, and we became partners."

"You're not married?"

"No. Not yet," replied Carson. After a moment he added

hesitantly, "I haven't got up the nerve to ask her yet."

"I see," John said, smiling when he saw that the other man was actually blushing. John looked away and hurriedly asked another question. "Is Mr. Taylor a family man?"

"He has a family, but not his own."

"How's that?"

"He and Mrs. Taylor have no children of their own, but she's one of a large local family, the Falcóns, so they have lots of nieces and nephews, as well as aunts, uncles, and cousins. You'll no doubt be meeting some of them while you're here.

"They're very nice people," Carson continued. "Mrs. Taylor's brother, Don Jorge Falcón, is one of our outstanding citizens. He owns a ranch out in the San Fernando Valley as well as a house in town. He also controls some of his wife's property south of here. She's a Carrillo, another of our local families.

"Doña Alma—that's Mrs. Taylor—also has a sister who was married to Alexander Aldon, a fine old California pioneer. He came here way back before the gold rush and settled on a beautiful place out east of here. Rancho Las Tunas, it was called, after all the cactus that used to grow there. *Tunas* are cactus fruit. I met Aldon a few times, when I first came out—a great old fellow! But he's dead now and most of the property was sold. I understand the widow would like to sell the last of it, if she can get a decent price. It's good land. If it were closer in, it could be subdivided and sold for homesites, but it's too far out for that."

"What kind of crops grow there?" asked John.

"Oh, everything: oranges, grapes, olives. Parts of it are even sheltered enough for lemons. Lemons can't take as much cold as oranges, but this land is right at the base of the San Gabriel mountains where it's protected somewhat."

"I remember seeing the name *Las Tunas* from the train as I

came in," said John. "Could that be the place?"

"That's it," answered Carson. "That depot is one of the improvements put in by the new owner, a man named Jonathan Lawson. He's even built a hotel and advertises for the tourists. I don't think he's had too much luck selling his lots so far, but he's got loads of money and plenty of other irons in the fire, and he can afford to wait. It's just a question of time."

"How much land does he have?" asked John.

"I don't know for sure, but I'd guess there must have been at least two thousand acres in the old Aldon *rancho,* and Lawson has most of it."

John said nothing further, but he made up his mind that one of the places he wanted to look at was the town of Las Tunas.

After a pleasant and substantial lunch at the Elite Cafe on Main Street, Steve Carson shook hands with John and went back to the hardware store, leaving John with Jim Taylor.

"Now, if you're not too tired, I thought we'd take a ride out through some of the farming areas—let you see some of our good land."

"I've seen several small vineyards and some orchards out on the edge of town," said John. "Carson took me quite a ways out."

"Well, we'll see some larger places this afternoon. I thought we'd go across the river and take a look at Boyle Heights and East Los Angeles. There's quite a settlement developing over there but still a lot of fine acreage. Then we'll drive down through Vernon—another new place—and back up to town from the south. I told my wife to expect us for dinner by seven, so we've got plenty of time."

The day was clear and beautiful, and a gentle breeze had

begun to blow in from the ocean. John would have been aghast had he known that the temperature was over the eighty-degree mark; in the east he would have been sweltering. Here in the shade of the buggy he was quite comfortable, especially after leaving the confines of the town behind, when he began to get the benefits of the rising breeze.

Taylor drove out of town along Aliso Street and across the river, where the street abruptly became a country road headed toward rising ground to the east. Within a short time John had seen a vineyard, an orange grove, and some fields of vivid green plants which he did not recognize.

"That's alfalfa," Taylor replied to his question.

"Alfalfa? Oh, yes, lucerne," said John. "I've read of it but never seen it."

"Makes the finest hay in the world," said Taylor.

"Better than clover?"

"At least as good as clover," replied Taylor, "and doesn't require as much water."

During the rest of the afternoon John saw other crops that were new to him: a field of chili peppers, a grove of avocado trees, and one of pecans, as well as the usual oranges and grapefruit. He also saw peach and walnut trees, as well as fields of corn, melons, and squash.

Occasionally they stopped to pass the time of day with local farmers, and in this way John met several transplanted easterners, an Italian, and a German.

Along about four o'clock Taylor pulled into the yard of a sprawling adobe ranch house belonging to a man Taylor introduced as Señor Ibarra. Here they were taken into the shade of a deep porch covered with bougainvillea where Señora Ibarra served tall glasses of cold lemonade and Señor Ibarra discussed the price of cattle.

Afterward they headed south, crossed the river again, and

drove through the newly subdivided town of Vernon. The "town" consisted of a crossroads with three or four commercial buildings and a dozen scattered residences, but there were signs advertising "prime commercial lots" and "choice homesites" on land that still showed the furrows of its former use.

A short time later Taylor turned the horse onto a well-traveled road labeled Alameda, and they headed north through another three miles of fields, vineyards and orchards, which brought them full circle back into Los Angeles again.

As they drove northward into the busy heart of the town, John was struck by the charm of the place. He was enjoying himself more than he had in years. But more than that, he realized with amazement, he was feeling a sense of homecoming.

CHAPTER FIVE

Taylor turned the horse into Fifth Street, passed Main, and pulled up before a small frame house on the north side of the street. A short, plump little woman came out onto the front porch as John was climbing out of the buggy, and hurried down the front walk, smiling as she came.

"Here's my wife," said Taylor. "Alma, this is Mr. Vanderburg. Show him inside while I take Molly around to the stable."

John removed his hat and smiled. "I'm glad to meet you, Mrs. Taylor."

"And I am so happy to meet you," she responded with just a trace of a Spanish accent and a frankly appraising glance from her dark eyes. She was a pleasant-faced woman of about fifty, with thick, dark, wavy hair parted in the middle and pulled into a heavy knot at the back of her neck. She gave him her hand with an old-world air of conferring a favor, then turned and led the way into the house.

The room they entered had all the typical-middle class furnishings of the time: a center table under an ornate hanging lamp, a platform rocker and an armchair near the table, a settee against the wall, and a whatnot in the corner. Yet at the same time John was aware of an indefinable foreign flavor. His eye was immediately caught by two large portraits hanging from tasseled cords above the settee.

Mrs. Taylor saw the direction of his glance and said, "My parents." The two simple words were spoken with a dignity and respect that reminded John of a Bostonian he knew saying "My ancestor who came over on the Mayflower." He looked again at the portraits and saw a very stiff, unsmiling, but aristocratic couple wearing old-fashioned and distinctly Spanish costumes. The man reminded John of the elderly gentleman he had seen on the station platform in San Bernardino.

"And which one do you take after, Mrs. Taylor? I do not see much resemblance."

She laughed with a quick toss of her head. "Ah, no! I think I am what you call a throwback. It has always seemed a great misfortune to me that I was not a tall, slim lady like my mother. My sister, Guadalupe, now, she is like her. But me, no.

"Do sit down, Mr. Vanderburg, and tell me about yourself. You are from the east, Jim tells me." Her pronunciation of her husband's name was not "Jim" or "Jeem" but an elusive something in between.

"Yes," he replied, "from New York City."

"Oh, yes?" she responded politely, and John had the feeling she would have made exactly the same response if he had said "Timbuktu."

"But now you will live here . . . when you have found a nice place." It was a statement, not a question. Clearly, there was no doubt in her mind. "Tell me where you went today. Did Jim show you what you wanted to see?"

"Why, yes, we saw all sorts of different farms and ranches. Mr. Taylor certainly outdid himself showing me around. It was very kind of him to neglect his business for my sake."

"Don't worry about that. You can be sure he enjoyed it as

much as you." Her dark eyes twinkled. "He was like a small boy let out of school when he came to get the buggy."

John began telling her of the things he had seen and the people he had met, enthusiastically recounting the details. She sat smiling and nodding, as genuinely pleased as he, until Taylor came in through the back of the house. Then she excused herself and disappeared into the kitchen, where he could hear her speaking in Spanish to someone—evidently a hired girl—against a background of kitchen clatter.

"Well, how about a drink before dinner?" said Taylor. "A little brandy and water?"

"That's fine," answered John.

When he had brought their drinks, Taylor settled back in the rocker and heaved a sigh of contentment.

"Here's to you. *¡Salud!,* as they say in Spanish. Means 'good health.' "

"Good health to you," said John.

"Tell me," said Taylor, "I've been wondering all day, how did a man like you, with your connections, decide to go into farming?"

It was a question John had heard time and again in the last few years. Usually he passed it off with a flippant answer such as, "I like the smell of manure," or, "I have a weakness for dairy maids." But something about this straight-forward man made him pause. James Taylor's honest friendliness and his pride in his state had impressed John during their long afternoon together, and he felt he owed him a straight answer.

"I'm not sure I can put it very simply," he said at last. "I've never really been interested in finance. I believe I began thinking about agriculture when I first visited our old family homestead in upstate New York. I was just a boy at the time, but it's a beautiful place, and I remember thinking what a shame it didn't make money so we could live on it. Of course, you understand that in our family—the male part, that is—making money is almost a religion."

Taylor nodded.

"There were some cousins living there at the time and they were not very well off. I remember my father was very patronizing to the cousins and could hardly wait to get back to the city. I didn't want to leave.

"After that I tried to get out of the city every chance I could. Of course we went to Newport every summer, but that wasn't what I wanted."

Taylor smiled. "I imagine not," he said.

"I went to visit an aunt," John went on, "who lives in Andover, Massachusetts. Her house is right in town, but it's a small community, and I could get out into the fields by walking a little, and I liked that. One year I talked the family into taking a vacation in Maine. We went to Bar Harbor, which wasn't exactly what I had in mind, but it was fun.

"Then, when I was in college, I spent one summer with a friend from Pennsylvania. His folks had a farm near Harrisburg and were well-to-do as farmers go. I really enjoyed that visit. But it wasn't until I went out to Chicago on the train that I began to think seriously that there might be money in farming. I'd never seen fields like those before—grain stretching as far as the eye could see, miles and miles of cash crops."

John paused reminiscently and sipped his brandy and water. "I did try to get interested in Father's business. I even made a stab at the social end of it. I'm sure you know that the business of finance is carried on as much in the homes of the men involved as in their offices. So I tried the social whirl—really worked at it.

"And *that,*" added John, "is really what finished me."

Taylor looked at him curiously. "How do you mean?" he asked.

"I couldn't stand it," replied John. "New York society is so false, so artificial—nothing but pretense. Many of the people we invited to our homes, and the invitations we accepted, were chosen strictly for financial advantage. Our whole way of life was based on money, and nothing's wrong with that, but we weren't supposed to admit it. We had to pretend to be above material things . . . so refined and cultured. I suppose the women are more responsible for that than the men. They don't know anything about business, and of course the men never discuss business in their presence, so it's no wonder they think money-making is vulgar—although they're perfectly willing to spend it.

"But there's more to it than that," John went on thoughtfully. "Everything we did was done in the name of culture—we discussed literature, attended concerts and the opera—and yet fashionable dress and expensive habits seemed to be more important to us than education or real moral worth. Almost any man can be accepted into New York society if he makes enough money and wears expensive clothing; but let him wear a suit five years old and live in the wrong part of town and it will not help that he holds three or four university degrees."

"I see," said Taylor.

"So," finished John, "I wanted out. Agriculture seemed an interesting and challenging way to do it." He took another sip of his brandy and water.

"And have you found it as satisfying as you expected?"

"Oh, yes," said John. "There's no question of the sincerity of a field of wheat, and there's no pretense about potato beetles or cabbage worms."

"That's plain," said Taylor, laughing, "but what about the people? Are you satisfied with the farmers you meet?"

"Well, yes and no," said John wryly. "I've met a few who

are fine straight-forward people. But I've also found some of the same sort of pretense, hypocrisy, and social snobbery, on a lesser scale, of course, that I tried to get away from."

Taylor nodded. "I believe you. I see the same thing right here in California. I saw it in New England, too. I'm afraid it's ingrained in a certain percentage of the human animal. But you just have to ignore that kind of people and search out individuals who look at life the way you do.

"Actually," he went on, "there are quite a few of us. We're just not as noticeable as the other kind. I imagine, if you think about it, you'll remember certain people in your New York crowd who didn't quite fit in with the others, who kept somewhat aloof from the group and didn't seem to worry too much what people said about them. I imagine if you went back now and looked around with an open mind you'd find some kindred spirits there—and everywhere."

"You may be right," John said thoughtfully. "Now that you mention it, I remember one fellow who is famous for saying exactly what he thinks. The ladies all consider him crude, but they're careful not to let him know it, because he's very rich. He congratulated me when he heard I had taken up agriculture, which I thought was odd, since all the others around me were shaking their heads and making dire predictions."

Mrs. Taylor appeared at that moment and informed them that dinner was ready. She led the men through an archway hung with velvet portieres into a small dining room where the table was set simply but elegantly with white damask, glassware, china, and silver. In the center of the table was a bowl filled with La France roses, and their scent mingled with the savory aromas of the food. The candles on the table remained unlit, since the room was bright with the golden light of the late-afternoon sun streaming in through a large bay window.

Lace curtains had been drawn back to catch the last of the ocean breeze.

John assisted Mrs. Taylor into her chair and then took the place set for him beside her.

"We saw the Ibarras today, Alma," said Taylor when they were all seated.

"Yes," replied his wife, "Mr. Vanderburg told me. How was Doña María? I heard she has not been well."

"She seemed fine today."

"What did you think of Rancho Las Flores, Mr. Vanderburg? Is it not a lovely place?"

"Rancho Las Flores?" echoed John.

"The home of the Ibarras."

"Oh! Yes, very lovely. Very nice people, too."

"They are old friends of Alma's family," said Taylor, passing a platter of meat to John. "Have some of this. I'm sure you'll like it. It's one of Alma's best concoctions."

John took a helping of the meat which appeared to be large chunks of beef prepared with a sauce of some kind. Upon tasting it, he found it to be mildly spicy with flavors completely new to him.

"That's delicious," he said.

The rest of the dishes were passed, finishing with a plate of fresh bread, and, after taking a slice, John passed the dish to his hostess.

"No, thank you," she said with a smile. "That is Jim's. I prefer my *tortillas,*" and she took something resembling a pancake out of a napkin in a basket beside her plate.

"What is that?" asked John.

"It's a *tortilla,*" said Taylor. "That's what the Californians use in place of bread. It's made out of corn and baked on top of the stove. They're fine for some things, but I still want bread with my meat."

"May I try one?" asked John.

"Of course," Alma Taylor smiled, handing the basket to him.

John removed a warm *tortilla* from the napkin and tore off a piece of it as he had seen Mrs. Taylor do.

"Take a little meat and gravy with it as you would with bread," she said.

John did as he was told. "Why, that's good!" he said. "What an odd flavor. A little like hominy, I think, but different."

Mrs. Taylor laughed. "We will make a *Californio* of you very soon! When you have found your *rancho* you will settle down and learn to eat *carne machaca* and *salsa verde*."

"He doesn't need to wait for that," said Taylor. "He can make a beginning on San Juan's Day."

"Of course!" cried his wife. "I almost forgot. You will go with us to my niece's house on San Juan's Day. We always have a big family party then, with a wide variety of food and drinks."

"When is San Juan's Day?" asked John.

"The twenty-fourth of June," said Taylor. "That's next Saturday. Today is the twentieth. Of course you must go with us."

"That's kind of you, but I wouldn't want to intrude on a family gathering."

"You wouldn't be intruding," protested Taylor.

Mrs. Taylor cast a reproachful glance at John. "If it were an intrusion, we would not invite you," she said. "In any case, the family would expect us to bring you, since you will be staying with us."

John looked at her blankly.

"Jim," she said, turning to her husband, "did you not tell him?"

"No, Alma," replied Taylor sheepishly; "I completely forgot. We were talking about farming and crops and a lot of other things."

"Tell me what?" asked John.

"That we expect you to come and stay with us while you are here. There's no reason why you should have to put up at a hotel when we have an extra bedroom."

"Why, that's really very nice of you, but my plans are still quite nebulous at the moment. I intend to be out of town most of the time, looking around. I probably won't even stay in town longer than tonight and possibly tomorrow night. I want to drive to some of the outlying districts and spend a night or two there in different locations. I'm not even sure when I'll be back."

Alma Taylor smiled. "That is all the more reason you should move in with us. You can come and go as you please, and if you want to leave your things here while you are away, you know they will be taken care of while you are gone."

"Well . . ."

"Just make this your headquarters," said Taylor. "We'll go down after supper and pick up your baggage."

The rest of the meal was leisurely and enjoyable. John warmed to these friendly people, and the longer he talked with them, the more at ease he became, as though he had known them for years. They discussed various locations where John might find suitable property. Taylor suggested the new Burbank area, and his wife mentioned San Gabriel and El Monte. John agreed to look at all of them.

After dinner John and Jim Taylor strolled down Spring Street to the Nadeau, where John collected his belongings and checked out of the hotel. He then hired a hack to deliver his things to the Taylor home, but since it was early and the evening fine, they decided to stop in the Nadeau's bar for a drink before walking home.

The bar seemed to be a gathering place for local businessmen, and John was introduced to several. Twice he was asked about his relationship to W. Stuyvesant Vanderburg, but he was accustomed to that, as well as to the sudden increase in cordiality that went with it. Taylor found the phenomenon highly entertaining; his lips twitched each time he observed it, and as they were walking home later he began chuckling aloud.

"What's so amusing?" asked John.

"People," replied Taylor. "I hope you realize that in the last half hour you've boosted my business and social standing more than I could have done by myself in ten years! Next thing you know, Alma and I will be hobnobbing with the Widneys and the Hellmans."

"It isn't me, of course," answered John, laughing. "It's my father. But you're more than welcome to any prestige you can get out of his name."

When they arrived home, Taylor recounted the story to his wife, laughing again, and Mrs. Taylor turned her dark eyes questioningly upon John.

"Is your father such a famous man?" she asked.

"He's very well known in business circles," answered John, thinking that here, at least, was one person who hadn't heard of W. Stuyvesant Vanderburg.

After John had arranged his few belongings in the upstairs bedroom overlooking the back garden, he came down again, and they all went out into the cool darkness of the front porch for a last quiet hour before bedtime. Taylor and John each lit cigars, and Mrs. Taylor worked on some knitting. In the quiet of the evening John could hear the slight rustling of palm fronds from a tree in the neighbor's yard, the chirping of crickets, and from somewhere down the street, the soft music of a guitar.

"Mr. Carson was telling me this morning"—was it only this morning?—"that the town has changed a lot in the last few years. What was it like before? What has changed?"

"Everything," murmured Alma Taylor.

"Yes, everything has changed," agreed her husband. "There are so many new people, for one thing—houses and farms everywhere. When I came here right after the war, it was still almost entirely grazing land, nothing but cattle ranches, and the town was just a few streets up around the Plaza. This area was farmland then. Alma was born here, of course. She remembers what it was like before the Americans came."

The couple began to reminisce about the town and its people, and with Taylor's dry New England humor and his wife's faint Spanish accent it was enthralling entertainment. Images began to form in John's mind of another world where proud Spanish families lived on great *ranchos* like feudal lords, where life was leisurely, and entertaining was frequent and lavish. The first Americans to arrive fell in with Spanish ways and were accepted into the system, becoming landowners in their own right, but as more and more easterners arrived, Yankee enterprise began to conflict with the casual indolence of the Californians, and the old, slow ways were gradually lost. John had glimpses of a small, dusty adobe town where cattle, dogs, and chickens ran loose in the streets, where banditry and hangings were frequent and gunfire in the saloons was commonplace—and all this in the very recent past. He began to think Steve Carson had reason to be proud of the new improvements.

When he finally said good night to his new friends and went up to his bed, he no longer had any question in his mind: He liked this country and wanted to stay here.

* * * * *

The following morning after breakfast, John accompanied Jim Taylor as he walked downtown to the hardware store. John had taken a lesson from the local people and was dressed in a less noticeable manner; not much less, however, since everything he owned was fashionable by Los Angeles standards.

"So you've decided to go out to Burbank today," said Taylor.

"Yes, I think so, even though I missed the big sale yesterday."

"Probably just as well. Those auction sales are always pretty wild. People get carried away. They'll buy in a hurry under pressure and are often sorry later. Of course," added Taylor, "many of them buy with the idea of reselling and turn right around and make a quick profit selling to someone else. I can hardly believe the way property values are soaring."

"By the way," said John, "Mr. Carson was telling me yesterday that Mrs. Taylor's sister has some property for sale in a place called Las Tunas."

"So she does, yes," replied Taylor. "I had forgotten that. It's only a small parcel, less than a hundred acres, but very good land, and a good location with plenty of water."

"I noticed the station name coming in on the train, and I've been planning on going out there in a day or so. If you'd give me a letter of introduction, I could call on her and look the place over."

"She's not there," replied Taylor. "She's here in town right now staying with her daughter. But there's no use in your approaching her anyway. Talk about a woman with no head for business! She can't even run her own household without help. Fortunately, she has daughters who have some sense.

"As far as the property goes, that's handled by her brother,

Don Jorge Falcón, but he's not in town right now. He's away on family business somewhere—San Diego, I believe Alma said. The Falcóns are a large family, and Don Jorge is the head of it since the old man passed away. That means he has to be a sort of advisor and business agent for the lot of them. He's always having to go here and there, helping a cousin or nephew out of trouble. He'll be back for San Juan's Day, though, and you can meet him then."

"In that case I'll just have to wait," said John. "However, it may be a day or so after that before I can see him. I hope Mrs. Taylor will forgive me, but I really don't think I will be able to attend her family party. I have so many places I want to see, and I'm afraid I'm going to run short of time. You see, my brother is arriving a week from today, on the twenty-eighth, and I'd like to have all my business taken care of before he gets here."

"Is your brother looking for property, too?"

"Oh, no. Just vacationing. He and my sister-in-law have been visiting friends in San Francisco. They'll want to do a little sight-seeing down here, and then we'll all go back to New York together."

"I see," said Taylor. "Well, in that case, of course, I understand you'll be busy."

"I'll explain to Mrs. Taylor this evening," John went on. "I'll be back early tonight, but tomorrow I want to head out into the country east of here, toward San Gabriel and El Monte and that place you told me about called Whittier. I don't expect to be back tomorrow night. I'd also like to see Anaheim and Santa Ana, and if I go down there, it will probably be Sunday, maybe Monday, before I can get back. I'll try to see Mrs. Taylor's brother then."

CHAPTER SIX

Taylor directed John to a livery stable where horses and buggies could be rented and John made arrangements for a week's use of a gig and a little bay mare answering to the name of Lolita. He was pleased with Lolita, but his tour of the Burbank area was disappointing. He spent a long day talking to everyone he met, and he thoroughly enjoyed the lunch Mrs. Taylor had packed for him, but the land he saw seemed more suited to grazing than farming. He returned to town later than he had intended and found that his hostess was keeping his dinner warm on the back of the stove.

The next morning, Thursday, he packed his smaller suitcase, and after explaining his plans once more to Mrs. Taylor, he said good-bye and walked to the livery stable to pick up his gig. San Gabriel was about ten miles out, and he arrived there before eleven o'clock after a leisurely drive by way of Mission Road.

He spotted a real estate dealer's sign almost immediately and was kept busy for two hours thereafter by a personable young agent with an easy smile and a flow of small talk. The man tried to sell him every piece of acreage he had listed, including a thirty-acre dairy farm, but after failing to arouse John's interest in any of them, he finally said a reluctant good-bye.

John ate lunch in a cafe across the street from the real estate dealer's office and asked the waitress how to get to El Monte.

"Just follow this street east," she told him, "until the road forks. Take the south fork."

John thanked her and left the town as directed. About a mile and a half east he came to the fork. A signpost with two arms stood at the junction. One pointed southeast and read EL MONTE. The other pointed northeast and read LAS TUNAS.

John halted Lolita and sat staring at the sign. Then he looked north along the road leading to Las Tunas. In the distance he could see the mountains he remembered from the train. The San Gabriels, Steve Carson had called them. They were blue and beautiful and they almost seemed to be calling him. His carefully planned itinerary suddenly lost its importance. He wanted to see those mountains up close.

"Well, why not?" he said aloud, and turned Lolita into the north fork. "I can go to El Monte tomorrow."

Late in the afternoon John entered the lobby of the Las Tunas Hotel. It was a typical country hostelry in the style of the day, standing back from the street in a large, landscaped yard. Upper and lower verandahs graced three sides of the building and a semi-circular drive led up to the front steps. John had tied Lolita to a hitching rail at the foot of the steps and walked up to the verandah and into the building.

The lobby was cool and dark and pleasant after his long drive in the heat, during which he had watched those compelling mountains grow steadily closer.

John approached the desk. "I'd like a room, please."

"For how long, sir?"

"For tonight—and possibly tomorrow night. I'd prefer

something on the north side."

"I have a second-floor room that's on the north, sir."

"All right, I'll take a look at it. Where is the livery stable?"

"It's right on the street behind the hotel. I can have a boy take your horse there for you, if you like, sir."

"No, I'll take her there myself after I've cleaned up a bit. I want to take a little walk before dinner anyway."

"Very well, sir."

John took out his watch. "What time do you serve dinner?"

"Between six and eight."

"Fine. That will give me plenty of time."

He took the key and his bag and climbed to the second story, where he located room 204. It was a typical hotel room except that the newness had not yet worn off the furniture, and the pattern of the carpet was still bright. The windows opened onto the upstairs verandah and offered a fine view of the mountains. The nearby slopes were very close and imposing here and more alluring than ever to John. *Wouldn't it be great to climb them?* He thought.

When he descended again to the lobby, he left the key at the desk, assuring the clerk that his room was satisfactory, and walked out across the verandah and down the steps to his gig. He drove Lolita around the hotel to the next street, where he saw barns and a corral about halfway down the block. Here he drove in and arranged for Lolita's welfare. Then, afoot, he began a leisurely tour of Las Tunas.

He walked south to the main street, turned east, and passed a brick grocery building he had noticed on his way in. There was a small dry goods store on the opposite corner with a barbershop next, and, after a vacant lot, another small frame building with a high false front. This last turned out to be an office bearing a sign, LAWSON DEVELOPMENT COMPANY, with another smaller sign in the window reading LOTS AND ACREAGE FOR SALE.

John spotted a young man at a desk inside and he came to a stop, but even as he stood hesitating, the young man got up from the desk, took down a hat from a hook on the wall, and prepared to leave. John pulled out his watch. It was a quarter to five. He replaced the watch and waited while the man closed up the office and came out onto the street.

"Mr. Lawson?" asked John.

The young man looked at John, took in his fashionable attire, and flashed a cordial smile. "No, sir, I'm Mr. Lawson's secretary, clerk, and general assistant. Willetts is my name," he said and he extended a hand to John.

"John Vanderburg," said John. "Glad to meet you. Will Mr. Lawson be in tomorrow morning?"

"Oh, yes. Mornings, he usually spends at least an hour in the office."

"Very good. I'll call in about nine, then. You can give him my card and tell him to expect me."

John handed him the engraved pasteboard, touched his hat, and moved off down the street to the east, while the other man stepped briskly to the main corner and disappeared around the dry goods store.

John strolled on past the last of the commercial structures and turned down a residential street, drawn by the prospect of a series of small, flower-filled yards such as he remembered seeing from the train. The houses in the yards were also small and unprepossessing, clearly belonging to people of limited means, but they were surrounded by a wealth of color and beauty in flowers, shrubs, and vines. The farther he walked toward the edge of the settlement, the poorer became the homes he passed, yet even here were bright beds of nasturtiums, geraniums, or other flowers, and many a tumbledown porch or precarious trellis was buried in roses. Dark-eyed children playing on the hard-packed dirt between the flower beds stared at him as he walked by, and he heard their excited comments in Spanish after he passed.

He turned eastward again, and the street he was on ended at the foot of a hill. He followed the base of the hill back toward the north and came to a pair of massive wrought-iron gates with the name *Lawson* worked into an overhead arch. Behind the gates a drive curved up the hill, and he caught glimpses of a sprawling adobe house at the top. The gates and drive struck John as pretentious and were clearly a recent addition to the much older house.

He turned away, and at the northern base of the hill he came again to the main street leading into the town. At this eastern edge of the settlement, the street had already become a country road bordered on the north side by a large orange grove. John headed back toward town.

At his table in the hotel dining salon a short time later, John ordered a steak dinner appropriate to the appetite he had worked up during his walk. He was served by a short, plump Mexican girl with heavy, dark braids tied up in loops behind her ears. She was much taken with John, and though her English left something to be desired, she made up for the deficiency by the tender manner with which she served his steak—or "es-stake," as she called it.

The dining room was more crowded than John had expected, most of the guests quite obviously tourists. There were two family groups, one with three small girls and the other with a teenaged son. Another group of three single women John mentally classified as school teachers on vacation. He also noted a young married couple and two single men—one middle-aged, whom John guessed to be a salesman, and the other a pale, thin fellow of twenty-nine or thirty, plainly tubercular. John smiled as he wondered how the others were classifying *him*.

Dinner over, he took a seat in the lobby, lit a cigar, and was enjoying his smoke when he was joined by the sickly young man he had noticed in the dining room. He turned out to be a bank clerk from Buffalo come west for his health, as John had surmised. He frankly admitted he had been drawn to John by the aroma of his cigar.

"I can't smoke the things anymore myself," he explained wistfully, "but a sniff or two of your smoke surely won't do me any harm."

They chatted for a while; then the young man excused himself, and John went out to the front verandah. Here he found the family with the little girls, all three running up and down the wide steps and climbing precariously on the railings. The mother and father, seated in the wicker chairs that furnished the porch, kept up a steady stream of admonishments.

"Be careful, Sarah! You're going to trip on those steps." "Get up, Belle, you're soiling your nice new dress." "Stop it, Baby, you'll hurt yourself." And so forth.

Seeking peace, John walked around to the north side of the building where he climbed an outside stair to the second-story verandah. This he found deserted, and he settled gratefully into a wicker rocker facing the mountains. While he finished his cigar, he watched the sunset shadows creeping across the canyons, sharply outlining their depths. The air was so clear that individual trees stood out on the tops of the ridges, still bright and golden in the last of the sunlight. The entire vista enchanted him.

"I must walk up to the foot of those mountains tomorrow," thought John. "After I've seen Lawson."

★ ★ ★ ★ ★

John's interview with Jonathan Lawson took up most of the morning. The man was a tall lanky New Englander with thin gray hair, tight-lipped and sharp-featured. After talking with him a few minutes, John suspected he was also tight-fisted and sharp in his business practices. He was, however, obviously impressed by the Vanderburg name and became as cordial as his bleak personality would permit.

He admitted, cautiously, that he had a few acres he might be willing to part with in exchange for some Vanderburg money, after which he took John into his buggy behind a magnificent gray gelding and proceeded to give him a tour of the Lawson domain.

John saw fields of grain, vegetables, and hay; he saw vineyards, groves, and orchards. He saw the irrigation system, including the main canal—or *zanja madre,* as Lawson called it—which brought the water from the mountains. Lawson explained the workings of the system as they were driving along a small branch canal where a laborer was directing the flow into the furrows of an extensive vineyard.

The worker looked up as they approached.

"¿Como le va, Juan?" asked Lawson.

"Bien, señor."

The vineyard extended on both sides of the canal, yet on the east side weeds and grass grew between the vines, while the furrows on the west, where the worker was irrigating, were clear and well tended.

"Why haven't these weeds been cleaned out?" asked John. "The vines appear to be healthy, bearing plants."

"They're not mine," answered Lawson curtly.

"Not yours?"

"No. This canal is the edge of my property. The land from

here to the mountains and about a quarter of a mile east belongs to a woman named Aldon. She's the widow of the former owner of the ranch."

"I see," said John.

"Unfortunately, her place is one of the best pieces around here, but you can see she doesn't take care of it. I'd get a hold of it if I could—you can see it's a natural extension of my land. I tried to buy it from her after her husband died, but she won't sell."

"Won't sell?"

"No. Just keeps it for sentimental reasons and lets it go to wrack and ruin."

Lawson's remarks surprised John but he made no comment. Either the man didn't know the truth, or he was lying. Looking at the fellow's cunning face, John suspected the latter.

After that, in the course of his tour, he saw a winery, a flour mill, and a tannery, all of which had plainly been built many years before and now stood idle and unattended.

"I have too many other interests to do justice to all of this," Lawson admitted, "and, besides, I'm not a farmer. I'm a businessman. But there's a fortune to be made here in subdivision."

Then he took John out toward the south, past fields where cattle and sheep were pasturing, to an area newly laid out in young orange trees. Here was another small extension of the canal system, where the water was running into the furrows. Beyond the ditch brushland extended in an unbroken expanse to a line of distant hills in the south.

"Someday this will all be cultivated," said Lawson, "subdivided into small farms. I'm making a start with these orange groves. People are learning that you can earn a comfortable living off a few acres of oranges. I've had inquiries already. I expect to make a nice profit on my investment," he finished smugly.

John remained noncommittal, but he admitted that he liked some of the areas he had seen.

"I'm looking at everything," he told Lawson, "but I'm not making any decision until after I've seen El Monte and the Santa Ana district at least."

Lawson nodded approvingly. "That's the way, young man. Never do anything in a hurry. I'll be around if you decide to stay in Las Tunas."

Lawson dropped John off at the steps of the hotel, oblivious to the stares of the tourists on the verandah. John mounted the steps and went immediately up to his room for the short time remaining before lunch.

When he appeared in the dining room a little later, he was the subject of rather more curiosity than usual because he had changed out of his fashionable suit and was dressed in rough breeches and hiking boots. It was the consensus of opinion among the ladies that he looked even more handsome than before.

After lunch he set out on a jaunt intended to take him at least partway up the side of those beckoning mountains. He wanted to get a view of the valley from up there. Lawson had driven him part way up a road that seemed to lead the way he had in mind, so he headed in that direction.

The road, hardly more than a track, led north from the east end of the main street of town, and John followed it happily, kicking up the deep dust like a small boy as he walked. He had not gone far, however, when he came to a heavily timbered bridge across the main irrigation canal. He remembered the bridge from his morning's drive. The road continued its dusty way on the other side, but John paused to watch the deep, quiet flow of the water.

Then he saw that there was a well-defined path along the margin of the canal. The path followed the canal as far as he could see and disappeared around a clump of bushes in the distance.

At once adventure called to John. He remembered Lawson's explanation that the water came from the mountains, and he was headed for the mountains, so why not take this route? He scrambled down the steep bank from the road to the pathway below and blithely made his way along the big ditch as it angled off to the northwest.

It was a pleasant walk and a beautiful day. The great mountains stood, tantalizing, in the near distance; the cool, flowing water was a reassuring presence beside him; and the wilderness of brushland stretched away on both sides. He decided that the brush was rather pretty, though certainly nothing like the green, verdant countryside of the east. He noted clumps of grass and wild flowers here and there. The large bushes which grew thickly around him were green—but it was a muted green, merging into the overall amber tones in the distance. Still, in its own way the view was a pleasing one.

He disturbed a family of quail with eight or nine little ones running in line behind the adults, and a few minutes later a rabbit leaped up almost beside him and scampered away. Up ahead the ditch curved and disappeared around a rock outcropping. Immediately he felt a surge of curiosity to see beyond it. Then he laughed at himself and began to wonder what it is in the human mind which always wants to see what is around the next bend or over the next hill. He concluded that most of us have a natural desire for something new and exciting that might lie just ahead, no matter how unlikely the possibility.

So he felt pleased as he rounded the curve to see that the

canal led into the heart of a grove of large trees; something new *had* appeared. He was wondering what kind of trees they were, noticing that they were not a natural growth but were planted in neat rows, when he first heard the whistling. He stopped a moment in surprise, but then walked on, concluding that some local boy was amusing himself in the grove.

The whistling was excellent, and the melody was a haunting, plaintive one. He slowed his steps to let the whistler finish his tune before intruding upon him, but the one flow of notes was barely finished before another was begun, and he kept walking on, so that the first John saw of the whistler was the clear view of a pair of puckered red lips pouring forth a Spanish melody. John stopped dead in surprise.

The girl did not immediately notice him, so John had a moment to take stock of her and attempt to control his disbelief. It was difficult. He had never in his life heard a woman whistle. And this was not ordinary whistling; it was music—clear, silvery, and true, graced with occasional little trills like those of a songbird.

She was seated on the ground, leaning backward, supporting herself with the bare palms of her hands, looking up into the trees over her head as she whistled; and she was splashing her feet—incredibly small white feet—in the water of the canal. John had never seen a grown woman with her feet and legs bare, nor had he ever seen one sit on the ground. Yet he was very much aware that this *was* a woman—a young, attractive woman.

She was wearing a blue calico dress with the full skirt pulled up almost to her knees to keep it out of the water, the sleeves rolled up above her elbows, and the neck open above the tight-fitting bodice. Her thick, glossy hair was fastened up onto her head, but damp tendrils of it were hanging down the nape of her neck and along her temples.

Suddenly she caught sight of him watching her and her whistle stopped abruptly. But the gaze she turned to him was level and unconcerned with no sign of shame or embarrassment. She lifted her feet from the water and calmly pulled her skirt down over her ankles, but she made no move to get up.

"Good afternoon," she said, exactly as though they had met on the hotel verandah!

John made a supreme effort: It was one of the tenets of his class that a gentleman never showed surprise, and the thoroughness of his training triumphed. He stepped forward and casually replied, "Good afternoon. Please forgive me if I startled you; I did not mean to intrude."

"How could you intrude?" she answered with a casual unlady-like shrug. "The path is open to everyone. The grove does not belong to me anymore."

The implication of her words passed completely over John's head. His mind was in such a state of shock that it was all he could do to dissemble well enough to meet his rigid standard of courtesy. He was trying desperately not to stare at her, but with every passing second he became more conscious that she was worth staring at. He would never have believed a woman so disheveled could be so beautiful. All his experience had taught him to think of feminine beauty in terms of the perfectly gowned and coiffed socialites of the New York ballrooms. He forced himself to look around the grove, at the trees and the sparse grass.

"What a pretty spot," he said, falling back on commonplaces as the only safe conversational ground.

"Yes," she said, gazing at the water.

"I . . . I suppose you live close by?"

"Not very close. A mile or so from here."

She must have walked all that way alone, thought John, filled with amazement, and at a loss for words.

He knew he should go on with his walk and leave immediately, but he desperately wanted to see more of this girl. He put his hands in his pockets and tried to think of some excuse for lingering. He had been following the path; she would expect him to keep on following it. Finally an idea came to him.

"I understood Mr. Lawson to say that this water comes from the mountains, and I was following the canal to see where it originates." He paused.

She gave him a sidelong glance. "You are visiting Mr. Lawson?"

"Oh, no. I'm staying at the hotel."

She turned then and looked directly at him as though seeing him for the first time.

"I was following the canal," he went on, "but it seems to continue for quite a distance. I think perhaps I'd rather not walk quite so far today." He tried to make his comment sound as casual as possible. "Would you mind if I sat down here to rest for a few minutes?"

He held his breath as he asked the question, acutely aware of her great dark eyes upon him. He half expected her to jump up and run away, as any other girl would have done at first sight of him; but she did not seem frightened by his unconventional request, or even nervous. Her breathing was perfectly calm, as far as he could tell. He stole a quick glance at her bosom, and the open throat of her dress revealed a strip of white skin where the golden color of her face and neck ended. He jerked his gaze back to her face.

"Of course I don't mind," she was saying with an incredibly sympathetic smile as an adorable dimple appeared and disappeared in her left cheek. "Sit down and rest. It *is* a very long way."

He sat down as close to her as he dared, and took a deep breath. Here, on a level with her, he had an even better view of her gracefully rounded arms and the soft curves beneath her tight bodice. And they *were* soft curves. It occurred to him that she could not possibly look so soft or sit as relaxed as she was if her clothing concealed the usual stiff shell other women always wore. Didn't even professional ladies of pleasure wear corsets when they went out? Surely she was not—? He threw another look at her clear, honest eyes and sweet, rosy lips. No, she couldn't be.

"Thank you, miss," he said. "It *is* miss—is it not?"

She hesitated an instant, then smiled. "You may call me María Anita," she said kindly.

John thought he understood: She had finally drawn a line of reserve, of propriety, and she did not want him to know who she was. Well, he would play the same game.

"And I am John Claremont," he replied, smiling.

CHAPTER SEVEN

When Anita had first realized who the young man was, she was swept by a wave of shock and sadness that such a fine-looking man, in the height of his youth and strength, should have been struck down by consumption. She remembered Emeterio saying that the sick fellow staying at the hotel had to walk for his health, and here he was, tired out by his exertions.

She saw a pair of wide-set gray eyes with the crinkles of laughter already marked at their corners; a square jaw below curving lips; and a clear, tanned skin. She was struck by the fact that he looked happy—and this affected her more than if he had been downcast: He had not lost courage in the face of slow, almost certain death. Pity welled up in her, and she lowered her eyes from his, lest he should see and be hurt by it.

She had almost told him that her name was Miss Aldon, but that had sounded so cold, and she wanted to be friendly even if it wasn't quite proper. What harm could it do to let this poor, sick man call her by her Christian name?

"What kind of trees are these?" he asked, looking around the grove as he spoke.

"They are eucalyptus," she replied.

"They are not native to the area?"

"No. They were imported into California from Australia,

but you can tell they like it here," she went on, dimpling at him. "See how big and healthy they are."

She lowered her eyes quickly, thinking she should not have mentioned health, but he turned to her, smiling.

"It seems everything does well here, including people."

"Oh, yes," she cried. "It is a *very* healthy climate."

She looked straight into those deep gray eyes of his for a moment and suddenly felt herself inexplicably drawn toward him. She glanced down at the water again until the sensation passed. He also turned his face toward the water.

"Yes," he said, a little absently, she thought. "I've seen an unbelievable variety of crops growing since I've been here—many more than we're able to grow in the east."

"You are a farmer, then?"

"Yes."

She wanted to ask where his farm was but thought it kinder not to remind him of a home he had had to abandon because of his sickness. She knew she would be miserable if she were ever forced to leave California. Instead, she said, "My father was a farmer, too. That's what he liked best."

"He is no longer living, then?"

"No."

"I'm sorry."

"That's all right. He died quite a while ago, and he was very old—almost eighty."

"Eighty!" exclaimed John. "Your father? Not your grand-father?"

"No," she replied, showing the dimple again. "You see, my father was already forty-four when he married my mother. They had a big family and I am the youngest. My sisters are much older."

"Forty-four is rather late to be married and start a big family. How did he happen to wait so long?"

"Oh, he was a confirmed bachelor and he had traveled all over the world. He told me he had never expected to marry at all, but when he met my mother she was so beautiful, he could not resist her."

"I understand," John murmured, looking down into her face.

"They met at a big party in Los Angeles, and he said no other girl there could compare with her."

"I can well believe it," said John. "And are all your sisters as beautiful as . . . your mother?"

"They say my sister Catalina looked just like her," replied Anita, "but she died when she was eight years old. My sister Adela is a little like Mamá—her coloring is the same—but most of us took after my father, especially me."

"Your father must have been a handsome man."

Anita smiled. "Thank you. That's kind of you. Yes, he was very distinguished. But as you can see," she added ruefully, "there is nothing distinguished about me."

A strange expression passed over his face, and he looked away from her, down at the water again. After a moment he said,

"That was a beautiful tune you were whistling as I came up the path. Was it a Spanish song?"

"As you came up? I'm afraid I don't remember which one you mean."

"It was rather plaintive, almost sad, and you whistled it beautifully."

She flushed with pleasure. "That must have been 'La Golondrina.' " She looked shyly at him from under her lashes. "Do you really think I whistle well?"

"It was beautiful! I've never heard anyone whistle that way."

"Don't you whistle?"

"Oh, yes, but not like that. Mine is just a plain garden-variety whistle, good for calling dogs and keeping ghosts away after dark."

She laughed. "Let me hear you."

"Well . . ."

"Do you know 'Love's Old Sweet Song'?"

"Of course."

He began whistling the popular song. After a few bars she joined him, harmonizing and adding little trills to his melody. He stopped in amazement at the full, rich sound of it.

"That's lovely!" he cried. "Let's try it again."

They started the verses again and this time went through the whole song to the end, she finishing with a little trill, a sort of coda, of her own. They looked at each other and laughed.

"We should go on the stage!" said John.

Her eyes were sparkling. "I never whistled with anyone before," she said. "What else do you know?"

John thought a moment.

"How about 'Nellie Gray'?"

"All right."

He began again, and she accompanied him as before, making an orchestration out of his simple tune.

"Why, that's beautiful!" he exclaimed again after the last notes had died away. He looked at her with undisguised admiration. "However did you learn to do that?"

"I don't know. I've been doing it for years when no one was around."

"Do that pretty Spanish one again," he said. "Could you teach it to me, please?"

She began the familiar melody, and he caught on to it quickly, and presently they were harmonizing on "La Golondrina."

"Oh, that is nice," sighed Anita. "Much better than whistling it alone."

They were smiling at each other and she was suddenly acutely conscious of his nearness to her. His presence was vital and magnetic, and when she remembered his illness, she could hardly accept it as a fact. She noticed his broad shoulders and muscular arms, one strong, shapely hand resting on his thigh as he sat beside her. What a tragedy that this glorious body was to be wasted away!

She had a sudden clear memory of Carlos Montenegro, one of her father's *vaqueros,* who had died of tuberculosis five years before. He had been thirty years old and had weighed less than a hundred pounds when he died.

Her smile faded, and she felt tears rising inside. She had not expected such an emotion. At least, she thought, she had given this young man a few minutes of forgetfulness. She bent her head to hide the brightness in her eyes and saw her bag of *yerba santa* leaves lying on the ground, reminding her of the passage of time. The pleasure of the last hour had made her forget everything else.

She reached for her stockings and shoes and began to pull them on, finding it a trifle difficult to keep her skirt modestly over her ankles as she did so.

"You are not leaving?" he asked.

"I think I should," she answered regretfully. "I have been forgetting the time, and I should be getting home." She stood up.

"This has been such a pleasure," said John, also rising. "May I walk with you?"

"We are not going in the same direction. I live over there,"—she pointed to the east—"and the hotel is down there," she said, pointing south. "Or were you still going to follow the *zanja?*"

"No," he said, "I only wanted to get a view of the valley from above. I thought if I followed the canal I might come to a place where I could look out over the town."

"Not the town," she answered. "The *zanja* curves around into the mouth of the canyon. To get a view of the town you would have to climb up on this side, and it is quite steep."

"Perhaps I will do that tomorrow."

"It is a very hard climb," she said doubtfully. "There is a trail farther east that would be easier."

He smiled, and the corners of his eyes crinkled. "You would have to show me where it is. Would you . . . could you do that? I'd be forever grateful to you."

"Well . . ." she said slowly, "not tomorrow. I will be away tomorrow. But I will be home again Sunday evening. And the day after that I might show you . . . if you will still be here."

"I will be here. When shall I meet you?"

"In the morning," she said. "That is the best time. Do you know where the big bridge crosses the *zanja?*"

"Yes, I came up that way."

"All right. I will meet you there, then, at nine o'clock, Monday morning."

"Until Monday, then," he said.

She held out her hand, and he took it eagerly in both of his own, bigger ones, holding it a moment before he released her.

"Good-bye," he said.

"Good-bye."

She started off down the path beside the water, but turned once and threw him a dimpled smile.

"Don't forget to practice 'La Golondrina'," she called, then turned and disappeared beyond the edge of the grove.

John waited a few quiet moments after she had gone, still filled with the wonder and thrill she had aroused in him. He was elated. She had promised to meet him on Monday! Forgotten completely were all his plans of touring the country; he thought only of Monday morning when she would meet him by the bridge.

He finally left the grove and started walking in the direction she had pointed out. He had perfect confidence that she knew what she was talking about, even though there was no path of any kind, and he was surrounded by wilderness. After about fifteen minutes he topped a low rise and saw a road a hundred yards beyond, coming from the northwest. He turned south when he reached it and followed it for some way before he finally made out the town buildings in the distance.

When he reached the hotel, he went up to his room and pried off his boots. He poured water from the pitcher into the bowl on the commode and washed his hot face. Feeling the grateful coolness, he thought again of little white feet splashing naked in the water of the ditch. The zan-ha she had called it. He remembered again the tantalizing glimpse he had had of graceful legs and trim ankles before she had pulled down her skirt. He stretched out on the bed with his hands behind his head and looked out at the mountains.

She was like the mountains, he thought—unspoiled and beautiful. *Natural*—that was the word. He thought it must be her naturalness that had so fascinated him. Even her name was soft and beautiful. María—what a pretty name it was. He had never heard it pronounced that way, much prettier than the American version.

He lay thinking of her until the shadows on the mountains began to deepen, and he realized the supper hour was approaching. He got up then and changed. He had originally planned on checking out of the hotel in the morning and driving down to Santa Ana by way of El Monte and Whittier. Now the trip did not seem necessary.

He realized that in the back of his mind he had already decided that he would buy some of Lawson's subdivisions and settle in Las Tunas. He had made the decision without concious perception. He was not yet ready, however, to admit to himself that meeting María had been the cause of that decision. He told himself that the land was good, the crops everything he was looking for. But he determined at least to drive down to El Monte and look around the following day. After all, he had two whole days to kill before he was to meet María again.

The thought of that meeting filled him with eagerness and he smiled.

As Anita walked home along the canal, the first pricks of conscience began. She had agreed to meet a strange man alone and unchaperoned. She could guess what her mother would say if she knew, and even Concha would be shocked.

Well, there was no need for either of them to know. She was not going to do anything wrong. She was merely showing a little hospitality, as a Californian, to the poor, sick, young man who was a visitor in her country.

She had always been somewhat contemptuous of all the rules laid down for the behavior of genteel young ladies. They were silly rules, she thought. She knew too well that many of the rules she had been taught did not apply to the working people of the community; but since her father had been the *patrón* of a large *rancho,* she was expected to show her "superiority" to the workers by maintaining a strict conformity to the rules of gentility. It made no difference that she was no longer rich; she was still of *la gente de razón*.

The rule against speaking with strange men—the definition of a *strange man* being one who had not as yet been properly introduced—was regarded by Anita as one of the silliest—almost as silly as the one against girls whistling. Twice she had had unpleasant experiences with men who had tried to become too friendly *after* being presented to her in perfectly respectable fashion. And since she had not been protected by the introduction but by her own awareness of the "gentlemen's" intentions, she had concluded that she herself was just as capable of judging strangers as were any of her older and supposedly wiser relatives.

So it was not the breaking of the rule itself that bothered her; she knew she was doing nothing morally wrong. The question that worried her was: Would *he* think she was being vulgar? Had she lowered herself in John Claremont's eyes by agreeing to meet him alone on Monday? She wanted very much for him to like her, though she did not ask herself why.

She thought over their encounter, and all the things he had said, with a glow of pleasure. He had not been appalled by her whistling; he had liked it. He had not appeared to be shocked by the sight of her bare feet in the water when he first arrived, although Anita was fully aware that such a display was considered almost indecent for a girl of her class. Servants might wear short skirts and show their ankles, but not ladies. Of course, she had covered her legs as soon as she had seen him, but still she knew that the people of her acquaintance would think she had compromised herself, and many men would have considered the whole situation an excuse for familiarity. On the contrary, John Claremont had treated her with every respect and dignity.

No, she did not think he considered her vulgar, and anyway, what difference did it make? She would see him only once more to show him the trail, and if he acted at all disrespectful, she would simply leave him at once and never see him again. For some reason, not seeing him again was an unpleasant thought, and she dismissed it from her mind. She had liked him, and she was certain he had liked her, too. She thought again of their whistling together and how much fun it had been. Mr. Claremont had enjoyed it as much as she had, she was sure.

Then she remembered his illness. Poor man, he deserved all the pleasure he could have while he could still enjoy it. Again she compared him with Carlos Montenegro.

Carlos had been a happy-go-lucky young man before the sickness took him. She had a child's memory of him dancing at the San Juan's Day fiesta when she was seven or eight years old. He had been the best dancer on the *rancho;* all the young girls wanted to be his partner. She remembered the girls flirting and Carlos smiling, and she remembered that she had wished she were old enough to dance with him. Then, as she grew older, a time had come when he was no longer able to join in the dancing at all, it would start him coughing, and she remembered him standing against the *patio* wall somberly watching the others enjoying themselves. After that he grew thinner each year until finally he was bedridden. And then he had died.

And this was the future for John Claremont! When she thought of his handsome, smiling face, it was almost impossible for her to accept his illness. Maybe it was possible that he would get well. She was sure she had heard that once in a long while someone recovered from consumption. *I will pray to the Holy Virgin for poor Mr. Claremont,* she thought. *Maybe she will take pity on him.*

CHAPTER EIGHT

Anita was not a religious girl. Her prayers were usually perfunctory, recited in a hurry without much thought and only when the occasion required it. But that night she prayed long and earnestly that John Claremont's life might be spared.

All the next day during the Fiesta de San Juan the thought of him stayed with her. On the long drive into Los Angeles, Emeterio and Concha did most of the talking, with Anita joining only occasionally in the conversation. Emeterio wondered if she were not feeling well because she was quieter than usual, and Concha openly scolded her for walking so much the day before and overtiring herself.

However, she did not appear sick. Emeterio thought she had never looked so well, and he felt an old man's pride in her youth and beauty. She was properly corseted and dressed in a tight-fitting gown of green silk trimmed with narrow bands of darker green velvet and cream-colored lace. The skirt was draped around her hips and caught into a cascade at the back, narrowed around her knees and flared at the bottom, creating the hourglass effect demanded by current fashion. Her hair was neatly piled atop her head, and a frivolous little straw hat covered with pink flowers and lace was tilted over one eyebrow. The hat was actually very firmly anchored by three gold hat pins, but it gave the fashionable impression of perching precariously.

It was ten o'clock in the morning when Emeterio pulled the wagon up before her sister's house on Fort Street in Los Angeles. Luisa's husband was a lawyer, Benjamin Wolfe, and their home reflected his affluence. It was an imposing two-and-a-half story brick edifice with cupolas and bay windows.

Luisa's oldest son, Benito, fourteen years old, hurried down from the porch to assist Anita out of the wagon. He was wearing a new suit with long trousers and was plainly trying very hard to maintain the adult dignity which the unaccustomed length imposed on him.

"Good morning, Aunt 'Nita. I am the official greeter today," he told her pompously.

"You, Benito? I almost mistook you for Silverio. How handsome you look."

"And you, too, Tía," he replied, gallantly offering his arm.

"Have they truly put you out here to welcome the guests?"

"Not really," he admitted, grinning, "but Papá and the uncles are in the library with Don Jorge, and Mamá is busy in the kitchen, and Mr. Thurber, Alice's new husband, is in the dining room with Mr. Carson and Enrique and Silverio." He lowered his voice. "They are supposed to be discussing politics, but really they are 'discussing' a very special jug of *bacanora*. Enrique brought it from Sonora when he was down there buying cattle for Don Jorge. So, you see," he concluded, his voice returning to normal, "all the men are busy except me."

At this moment two little six-year-old girls, Anita's nieces, came running around from the side yard, squealing happily. They began a running commentary almost simultaneously:

"Tía Anita! Tía Anita! We knew you must be here when we saw Emeterio! See our new dresses, Tía? Don't we look nice? And this is Adelita's new doll—she got it on her birthday." "Kitty got a new doll, too, though it was not her birthday, but she is so little, Papá bought her one anyway." "Come upstairs and let us show you Tía Elena's new baby. He is so beautiful and fat."

"Wait! Wait!" cried Anita, laughing. "You have neither one kissed me yet. Here, Lupita," she said, bending down, "and here, Adelita . . . Now," she added, straightening up again, "before I go to see the baby I must greet Doña Carmelita and Doña Alma and pay my respects to Don Jorge and Uncle Jim."

"There is somebody else for you to greet, too, Tía," cried little Lupita. "Guess who else is here!"

Adelita turned accusingly to Benito. "You have not told her, have you?"

"How could I tell her?" protested Benito. "You two don't let me get a word in edgewise."

"Well, then," asked Anita, smiling, "who is here?"

"It is Grandma's sister Luz," said Adelita.

"Only she says they call her Sister Angelica," put in Lupita.

"That's all right," added Benito, "we will still call her Tía Luz."

"Well!" exclaimed Anita. "That is a surprise! She has come a long way." Her mother's youngest sister, Luz, was a Dominican sister at the convent in San José, and Anita had not seen her for six years. "Come then," she said, grasping a hand of each child, "take me in to greet everyone."

In this way she was led proudly by her two small nieces into the parlor, where the aunts were seated in mature dignity exchanging family gossip. The nun, Tía Luz, sat between Anita's mother and Doña Carmelita Carrillo de Falcón, wife of Don Jorge Falcón, and her plain white robes and dark headdress provided a stark contrast to their colorful silks.

"Ah, María Anita!" exclaimed the nun, leaping to her feet and taking Anita's face in her hands. "Can it really be you? So grown up! I expected it and yet I can hardly believe it."

"And you, Tía," said Anita after kissing her aunt. "You are just the same. You never change."

"Well, why should I change? I live the life of God in continual peace, not like Guadalupe here, who has watched her loved ones die and her fortunes dwindle; or like Jorge, who has so many responsibilities and has become so stiff and dignified. I would hardly have known he was the same brother who used to tease us about flirting with the boys when we were young. Do you remember, 'Lupe?"

"Yes, yes," murmured Anita's mother.

"Did he tease you, too, Tía Luz?" asked Anita. "I thought you were always too serious to think about boys."

"I was serious, yes, but there were one or two . . ." She smiled reminiscently.

"Did you not know, Anita," put in Doña Carmelita, "that Don Jaime Salvatierra would not have married Doña Isabel if Luz had not taken the vows?"

The nun laughed. "Poor Jaime!" she said, "he thought he loved me, but I do not think he has missed me. He was not like Don Alejandro. If *you* had taken the vows, 'Lupe, *he* never would have married."

Guadalupe Aldon smiled sadly. "Yes," she murmured, "Alejandro loved me. One of the things that killed him was seeing me reduced to nothing on our own *rancho.*" She paused, then brightened and became animated. "Oh, but Anita! You have not heard the news!"

"What news, Mamá?"

"We may be moving to town soon!"

"What do you mean?"

"There is a very rich man in town from the east who is

looking for property, and he has asked your uncle Jim especially about our land."

"But he has not seen it yet," said Anita. "He may not like it."

"Oh, I am sure he will like it. Why should he not? He is going to talk with Jorge in a few days and then he will come out and look over our place. He has lots and lots of money and can pay us a decent price, not the pittance that old Lawson offered us." She tossed her head contemptuously. "Just think, Anita," she went on, full of enthusiasm, "we will be able to buy a nice house in town and be near the family instead of stuck out there in the country where nothing ever happens."

"Well, perhaps," Anita said cautiously, "but let us see if he likes our land first, and how much he offers for it. Mr. Lawson has plenty of money, too. He could have offered more than he did. This man may be just as tight as Lawson."

"Oh, no, he is not," insisted Guadalupe. "Talk to your uncle Jim. He knows all about it."

"When I see him, I will ask about it," replied Anita, "but I have not yet had a chance to talk to Doña Carmelita. How are you, Tía?" she asked, turning to the other aunt. "You look well."

"Oh, yes, I am well, finally."

"Have you been ill?"

"Last week, yes. I was perfectly miserable. It was Enrique's fault. He caught the grippe on his trip home from Sonora. That is what comes of sleeping on the ground at night! Of course I had to catch it from him, and Ofélia, too. You know Ofélia is so delicate. She is like me; she catches everything."

"María did not catch it?"

"Oh, no! That María is like a horse! She takes after Jorge,

and so does Silverio. Would you believe Silverio and María were mean enough to laugh at Ofélia and me because our noses were red and our eyes watering?"

"I would believe it of Silverio—it sounds like him—but I would not have thought María would be so mean."

"It is the truth. But I got even with her. I said, 'María Concepción, how dare you laugh at your own mother? Wait until I tell Mr. Carson how disrespectful you are. He will not think you are so perfect then.' That stopped her! She said, 'Oh, Mamá! You wouldn't do that!' "

"Mr. Carson?" asked the nun. "The partner of Alma's husband? Is he interested in María Concepción?"

"Oh, yes," replied Doña Guadalupe. "He has been in love with her for more than a year, but he is so bashful, he can hardly say a word in her presence."

"It does not seem possible she is old enough for suitors," sighed Luz.

"She is eighteen," protested Doña Carmelita. "I was sixteen when Jorge and I were married, and Enrique was born when I was eighteen."

"And my granddaughter, Luisa's girl, Alice, is only seventeen," added Anita's mother, "and she was married last April."

"That is right," murmured the nun. "I forget. I am so far removed from all these things, I cannot keep track. What about you, Anita? Who is your admirer?"

Anita shook her head.

"I do not have any admirers, Tía."

"What! Not any? As pretty as you are? I do not believe it."

"It is her own fault, Luz," Doña Guadalupe interposed. "She will not try to attract any young men. She will not listen to them respectfully, but talks to them directly and boldly as if she were another man! She will not act feminine and helpless to make them want to protect her. I tell you, she frightens them off!"

The nun's eyes twinkled. "Is that true, Anita?"

"Yes, Tía, I am afraid it is. That is the way I am, and it does not seem right to pretend to be something I am not."

"Well, Niece," said the nun, smiling, "I agree with you. It is always better to be honest."

Anita's mother shook her head in annoyance. "That is all very well, Luz," she protested, "but *you* live in a convent. If Anita wants to go into a convent, I will have nothing to say, but if she is going to live in the world of men she must learn to please them."

"Oh, 'Lupe," put in Doña Carmelita, "don't worry yourself so! Anita has not yet met anyone she likes. When that happens it will be different. She will want to make herself pleasing then."

A sudden memory of John Claremont came to Anita as her aunt spoke, and with it a soft surge of the sadness.

"You may be right, Tía," she said quietly. "But speaking of pleasing the men, I have not yet been to see my uncles. I had better go find them. Benito said they were in the library."

"Yes, I believe so," said Doña Carmelita. "Run along, my dear. They will want to see you."

Anita was met at the hall door by Lupita and Adelita, the two small escorts who had been waiting impatiently. Together they made their way to the library, a large pleasant room with deep comfortable chairs, walls lined with books, and a marble fireplace, cleaned for the summer and concealed by a brass screen.

Standing before the mantel, his hands behind his back, was her uncle, Don Jorge Falcón, a dark, portly man in his late fifties. Beneath graying temples, his aristocratic face was accented by a long, straight nose—the falcon's beak, as it was called by local Americans.

Opposite him in leather chairs sat her uncle, Jim Taylor, and her brother-in-law, Benjamin Wolfe. At the big bay window stood her other two brothers-in-law, Tom Gooden, a local mason, and Marcus Goetzler, a grocer from Santa Barbara, both men under forty.

Lupita immediately dropped Anita's hand and ran across to Benjamin Wolfe, calling as she ran. "Look, Papá! It is Tía Anita finally arrived. Isn't her dress beautiful?"

"Yes, yes, my child, very beautiful," replied her father as he and Jim Taylor stood up to greet Anita. "But you are making an appalling amount of noise; you must lower your voice."

Anita turned first to Don Jorge, who stepped forward to embrace her in the Spanish manner.

"Ah, María Anita!" he exclaimed in genuine pleasure. "*¡Qué dichosos los ojos!* What a pleasure to see you! And the child is right; that is a lovely dress."

"*Gracias,* Tío," she replied, then turned to shake hands with Benjamin, Tom, and Marcus, who had come forward to greet her.

"Well, little sister," said a smiling Gooden, "I see Adelita has latched on to you already. She has talked of nothing all week but seeing Tía Anita."

"She and Lupita are chaperoning me," replied Anita, smiling.

"That's fine," he said to Adelita, "but you must not bother your aunt too much, youngster. When she is tired of your antics, you must leave her alone, do you hear?"

"Why, Papá!" protested the child in a tone of injury, "I wouldn't bother Tía Anita. We are not bothering you, are we, Tía?"

"No, of course not, dears."

She turned to Jim Taylor, who had stood smiling broadly during this exchange, and now came forward to give her a kiss on the cheek.

"Good to see you, my dear."

"And you, too, Uncle Jim. But please tell me, what is it you have been saying to Mamá about someone wanting her property to get her so excited? She is as good as moved to town in her imagination."

Taylor laughed. "I'm sorry, Anita. All I did was tell her about my visitor from New York. His name is Vanderburg, and he is the son of W. Stuyvesant Vanderburg."

"The millionaire?"

"That's right. The son is out here looking for property to buy. I've been showing him around and he asked me about your place. Steve Carson evidently mentioned it to him first. I referred him to Jorge, here, and he'll probably want to come out and look it over after he gets back from Santa Ana."

"Did you tell him how small it is? Surely he will want a whole *rancho,* not just a little piece like ours."

"Yes, I told him, but he still wanted to see it. Of course, he may find something he likes in the Santa Ana area. We won't know until he gets back."

"Well," said Anita thoughtfully, "let him come, but I will not start packing up to leave yet."

Lupita tugged gently on her skirt. "Come, Tía, you have not seen the baby yet."

Anita glanced at Marcus Goetzler. "They are very insistent that I admire the new little Goetzler, Marc. Where is Elena? Is she with him?"

"Yes," replied Goetzler. "She went upstairs to feed him a short time ago."

"Then we will go up, too. But," she added to the two little

nieces, "you must promise to be very quiet in case the baby is asleep."

"Yes, Tía," said Lupita. "We promise," added Adelita. The answers were simultaneous but solemn.

The promise proved unnecessary. Upstairs in the big front guest room Anita found her sister, Elena Goetzler, and the baby surrounded by all the teenaged girls of the family. Elena was the mature mother of three small sons, but still retained her interest in the affairs of the younger generation. There was much talk and laughter, and four-month-old Rudolph was being passed around from one relative to the other with every sign of pleasure on his fat little face. Alice Thurber, the recently married daughter of the house, was in current possession when Anita and the little girls joined the group, but her right to keep holding him was being loudly questioned.

"Come, Alice, let someone else have a turn," begged María Luisa Gooden, a blonde of fifteen, who was always called by both names to distinguish her from María Anita and María Concepción, the older Falcón girl.

"Yes, do," urged Ofélia Falcón. "After all, you will probably be having one of your own, soon."

"Ofélia!" cried her sister. "What a thing to say!"

"Well, why not? She's married, isn't she? You *will* be having one, won't you, Alice?"

"I hope so," replied Alice, blushing.

"Of course you will," insisted Ofélia. "So give Rudy to me. *I* will not be married for years and years."

"How silly you are, Ofélia," said her sister, María Falcón.

"Well, here is Anita," said Alice, "and she will want to hold him, too, so I may as well give up. Here he is, 'Nita. Isn't he a little doll?"

"So this is my newest nephew!" said Anita, holding him at

arm's length for a critical inspection, then giving him a hug and kiss. "Well, he is worth waiting four months to see! What a sweetheart! Is he always this happy?"

"Oh, no," Elena answered truthfully. "I have to admit he was very fussy on the trip down, but he likes all this attention. His brothers don't play with him much yet."

"When did you arrive?"

"Last night. We were late for supper but Luisa had saved us some leftovers."

"It is so good to see you again! I wish you did not live so far away. Oh, could somebody please hand me a towel or something to put over my dress in case Rudy has an accident."

"Give him to me," insisted Ofélia, "and then you won't have to worry."

"No, it is my turn," said María Luisa.

"What about me?" added the other María.

"Listen to them!" exclaimed the baby's mother. "I am going to take him away from all of you in a minute. It is time he had a nap."

"Here, then," said Anita, handing the baby to her sister. "I want to take my hat off and go down to see if I can help Luisa. Am I to stay in the other guest room with Mamá?"

"No, no, Tía!" cried little Lupita. "You are going to stay with me in my room. Tía Luz is with Grandma."

"Oh, of course. I forgot about Tía Luz. You won't mind sharing your room with me, Lupita?"

"Oh, no, Tía."

Adelita, on Anita's other side, was pouting jealously. "I wish you could come and stay with me at our house."

"Some other time I will, dear."

"You don't have room for her!" protested Lupita. "Your house is too small, and your room is just a little one, not nice and big like mine. Besides, Kitty has to sleep with you."

"Hush," said María Luisa. "There is plenty of room for Anita at our house. She can sleep with me and not disturb Kitty. Next time she can go there."

Adelita's face brightened, and Anita smiled her thanks.

A little later, Anita and María Luisa walked downstairs together leaving the children behind with the baby.

"Have you met Silverio's friend yet, Anita?" her blond niece asked.

"No. What friend?"

"The friend Silverio brought with him today. He's visiting from Baja California, and he's very handsome. His name is Antonio Valenzuela." She lowered her voice. "I think he was quite taken with María. When Silverio introduced him to her, he kissed her hand, and you should have seen Stephen Carson glaring at him!" Then she added, "Señor Valenzuela didn't offer to kiss *my* hand."

Anita smiled at the comment. "Poor Mr. Carson," she said. "Why do you suppose he has not proposed to María? Everybody knows he is crazy about her."

"María says he is always embarrassed when they are together," confided María Luisa, "and he doesn't say much of anything to her. But let us go slowly past the dining room door and maybe you can get a look at Silverio's friend. Oh, no, they are not there. They must have gone out to the garden."

"We will see them later," said Anita without much interest. Silverio's taste in friends seemed to her to be consistently bad. One of them had been particularly obnoxious at Christmastime. "Anyway," she went on, "I must find Luisa and Doña Alma and see if there isn't something I can do."

"Oh, but wait a moment!" cried the younger girl, laying a

hand on her arm. "Have you heard about Doña Alma's houseguest?"

"Houseguest?"

"Yes. The rich man from New York."

"Oh, him. Yes, but I didn't know he was staying with Aunt Alma and Uncle Jim."

"Yes! And I would just love to meet him! Aunt Alma says he's very nice and young and handsome. Of course, you'll get to meet him because he wants to look at your land, but I suppose it will be just my luck that he'll go back to New York before I get a chance to see him."

"Well, I may not see him, either," laughed Anita. "I suspect he will find a big ranch down around Santa Ana and will never bother to look at Mamá's little eighty acres. But if I do see him," she added, "I will be sure to describe him to you."

CHAPTER NINE

Anita found her sisters, Luisa Wolfe and Adela Gooden, in the kitchen with Doña Alma Taylor, as well as old Concha, who was already hard at work assisting Luisa's cook, Carmen.

Luisa and Adela were both handsome, capable women in their thirties who had been married and settled in Los Angeles for as long as Anita could remember. More like cousins to her than sisters, they were not as close to Anita as Alice or María Luisa, their daughters. They greeted her warmly but not as affectionately as Doña Alma Taylor, who had a special fondness for this particular niece.

"Anita *mía,* I have been waiting for you to make the *salsa,*" said her aunt, giving her an embrace, "but are you sure you want to do it in that dress? It is so beautiful, it would be a shame to soil it."

"Thank you, Tía. Do you not recognize it? It is made from the silk you and Uncle Jim gave me last Christmas."

"So it is! Who made it up for you?"

"There is a new dressmaker in Las Tunas. She is the wife of the Santa Fe ticket agent."

"Well, she has talent. Maybe I will come out there to see her myself."

"Give me an apron, Luisa, and I will start the *salsa.*"

"Well . . . if you are sure. Your *salsa* is the best in the family."

"It is Concha's recipe," protested Anita.

"No es verdad, mi hijita," said Concha. "That is not true. You added some *verdolaga* and a bit of *yerba buena* to my recipe, and the flavor is much better than mine."

Enveloped in a voluminous apron Anita set to work, and the morning passed pleasantly. After a while María Falcón came into the kitchen, and Luisa put her to work also.

"Go into the dining room, please, María, and see how much of a mess the young men have left with their glasses and cigar butts. We will have to get it all cleaned up before we can start laying the table."

María went out and a short time later brought back several used glasses. Concha poured hot water into a dishpan and began to wash them while María made a second trip to the dining room.

Anita finished the *salsa* and was left with nothing to do when Elena came downstairs and appeared in the kitchen, saying the baby was asleep. Luisa took the apron off Anita and put it on Elena.

"I'm almost ready to start rolling the *enchiladas*. You can dip the *tortillas* for me while Carmen fries them. Anita, see what is taking María so long. You can help her with the table if she needs it."

Anita went out into the dining room. It was dark and cool after the heat and brightness of the kitchen, and at first she did not see the couple in the corner by the sideboard. Then she realized it was Stephen Carson standing beside María and looking very embarrassed.

"Oh, hello, Mr. Carson," she said, trying to sound as casual and unconcerned as possible. "How are you today?" And she hastily turned away from them and began collecting some ashtrays off the dining table.

"Uh, fine, just fine," stammered Carson. "I, uh, was just asking Miss Falcón if there was anything I could do to help . . . but I guess there isn't." He took a step back from María and threw a glance at the hall door. "I'd better be going," he went on. "I don't want to bother—I know you're busy." He gave María a last longing look and started toward the door.

Anita had an inspiration. "Perhaps you *could* help, Mr. Carson, if you're sure you don't mind?"

He paused in his progression toward the door and Anita gave him a quick smile. "Luisa would like some flowers cut for the table and I'm much too busy to do it. Would you mind helping María cut some roses out in the garden?"

Carson brightened perceptibly. "I'd be happy to," he replied.

María's gaze had been on the carpet, but she now gave Anita a questioning look.

Anita stepped up to the sideboard directly in front of María, gravely winking at her as she did so. "I believe Luisa keeps some shears in here," she said, pulling out a drawer and rummaging through it. "Yes, here they are."

María took the shears with a grateful little smile. "We'll need something to put the flowers in," she suggested.

"Yes," agreed Anita. "Well, a sheet of newspaper will do, I guess."

"Oh, wait," said María, "I know what Luisa uses. There's a basket in the hall closet."

"Fine," said Anita. "Mr. Carson can pick it up on the way out."

Anita gave Carson a final smile and María a pat on the shoulder as they went out into the hall together. Then she turned to the table and finished clearing it off. When it was clean, she got a linen tablecloth out of the sideboard and spread it over the mahogany, then took two silver candlesticks off the sideboard and set them on the table.

Back in the kitchen, Anita was put to work again and kept busy for quite a while. She did not see María when she returned with the flowers, but she heard her sister Adela telling Luisa that the roses on the dining table were beautiful.

"What roses?" asked Luisa.

"María picked them," said Anita.

"María Concepción?"

"Yes."

"That was nice of her," said Luisa.

"And she has arranged them beautifully," added Adela.

Soon after that the food was declared to be ready. Carmen and Concha began spreading everything out on the dining table and on the sideboard, while the ladies of the family went upstairs to freshen up.

Anita was smoothing up the stray ends of her hair before the mirror in Lupita's bedroom when María Concepción came into the room. She was full of suppressed excitement and she closed the door behind her before speaking. Then she burst out happily, "Oh, Anita! Thank you, thank you! It worked. I'm so happy!"

Anita turned to her cousin. "You mean he really did it? He proposed?"

"Yes! Yes! Oh, Anita, he'd never have done it if you hadn't sent us out into the garden. How did you ever think of it?"

"I don't know," Anita replied truthfully. "It just seemed like a good idea. He looked so desperate. I could see he didn't want to leave you, but he needed an excuse to stay with you, so I gave him one."

"It was perfect, Anita, just perfect! When he came into the

dining room, I could tell he wanted to speak, but you know he is so bashful. And I couldn't find an excuse not to look at him."

"What do you mean 'not to look at him'?"

María giggled nervously. "Well, I know this sounds silly, but I found out—oh, a long while ago—that if I looked right into his face, he couldn't say a word. He'd shut right up, even in the middle of a sentence, and just stare into my eyes. But if I was busy doing something and looking at my work instead of him, he would talk into my ear and say all kinds of things." She sighed. "Twice I thought he was going to tell me he loved me—I'm sure he started to—but then I looked up into his face, and he just couldn't speak."

"But he spoke today?"

"Yes! Oh, yes. I was cutting roses, you see, and I made up my mind I would keep looking at the roses as if he were not there at all. Oh, I would say something once in a while, of course, but I never looked at him once until he got it all out and asked me if I'd honor him by becoming his wife. And *then* I just looked up at him and said 'yes' . . . and . . . and he didn't need to say anything more."

Anita began to laugh, and María joined in, but her laugh turned to a sob.

"I'm . . . not sure if . . . I want to laugh . . . or cry," she stammered, as her voice broke and tears came into her eyes. "I've been so afraid . . . so unsure . . . and now I'm so happy!"

"And I'm happy for you," Anita assured her, putting an arm around her. "Have you told anyone else?"

"He wants to speak to Papá, himself, first."

"Good heavens," said Anita, "you don't supposed Mr. Carson will be tongue-tied with *him,* do you?"

"Oh, no," answered María. "He never has trouble talking to men. Only to me."

Anita laughed again. "Don't worry. He'll get over that, now," she said.

The rest of the day passed pleasantly and yet a little sadly for Anita. While everyone else was gay and happy, poignant thoughts of John Claremont would often trouble her. This always seemed to happen when everyone was laughing the loudest. She would suddenly remember that not everyone had as much cause for joy as she and her family.

María Falcón, of course, and her Mr. Carson were among the happiest, now that the course of their true love had finally run smooth. Carson could even look on complacently while Señor Valenzuela, Silverio's friend, made gallant remarks to María; and sometime during the afternoon—Anita was not sure when—he contrived to take Don Jorge aside and speak to him. Anita did see Don Jorge, all smiles, approach his daughter and embrace her, and she at once concluded he had approved the match.

The event was not generally known, however, until evening after the musicians had arrived and everyone was gathered in the back garden to listen and sing. At last Don Jorge stood up before them all and announced the engagement, and there was much cheering and well-wishing. Even Señor Valenzuela put a good face on his discomfiture and congratulated Stephen Carson as though he really meant it.

Anita's mother, standing beside her during the announcement, sighed deeply. "Now you see, Anita, your cousin will be married before you, and you the older of the two! Why couldn't you have been less of a hoyden? Mr. Carson could just as easily have fallen in love with you instead of María. But you are always too bold, not shy and feminine as she is."

"Oh, Mamá! How can you say such a thing? I would not

have wanted Mr. Carson to fall in love with me. He is not my kind at all."

"Clearly, you are not *his* kind!" her mother responded petulantly. "He is a fine, hardworking young man and will give María Concepcion a good home. But what will become of us when you are an old maid and we are dependent on our relations to take care of us?"

Anita did not answer, but she thought it might be no worse to be dependent on one's relatives than on a husband one could not love.

"I do not understand you, Anita," her mother went on. "Look. There is Silverio's friend from Baja California. They say he owns property near Ensenada, and he's quite good-looking, yet you have not even tried to attract him."

Anita looked at Señor Valenzuela, who was standing with Enrique Falcón while his bold eyes roamed over the gathering, lingering on each and every feminine form in the garden. She shuddered.

"¡Santa Madre!" she muttered under her breath. "Being an old maid would be preferable."

At that moment the musicians struck up "La Golondrina" and Anita began to sing with the others. But suddenly tears stung her eyes, and her words were choked off by a constriction in her throat. She turned away from her mother and walked quickly to a table at one side where pastries and candies were laid out. She bent her head over the dainty rolls and pretended to be deciding among them while she composed herself. Finally she selected a candy and walked off with it into a shadowy corner, where she threw it under a bush and then dabbed at her eyes with the lace edge of her sleeve.

After the song had ended and the musicians began a lively dance tune, she emerged from the shadows and, seeing her

Aunt Alma and her Uncle Jim sitting together under an arbor, quietly joined them.

"There you are, Anita *mía,*" said Doña Alma, moving over to make more room for her. "I wondered where you were. I always listen for your voice when they play 'La Golondrina'—it is such a favorite of yours; but this time I didn't hear you."

"My mouth was full," lied Anita.

"Isn't it wonderful about Mr. Carson and María?" said Doña Alma. "Jim is so pleased."

Jim Taylor smiled. "Best thing in the world for Steve and the business. Nothing like having a good wife to make a man want to succeed. I know," he finished, taking his wife's hand in his and smiling into her eyes.

"I hope they will be as happy as you two," Anita said sincerely.

"Yes," Doña Alma agreed. She smiled at her husband. Then, looking again toward the musicians, she said: "Isn't it a shame, Jim, that Mr. Vanderburg couldn't be here?"

"Sure is," agreed Taylor. "He'd have enjoyed it, I know."

"You invited him here?" asked Anita in surprise.

"Of course," said Doña Alma. "He is our guest."

"And a fine young man," said Taylor.

"I can't imagine he'd have much in common with us," said Anita. "I'm not surprised he didn't come."

"What do you mean, Anita? Our people are the best in the world," said her aunt naively.

"Of course, but *he* might not think so."

"No," put in her uncle, "he's not like that. He's just as open and friendly as you are. Why, Enrique puts on more airs than Vanderburg does, doesn't he, Alma?"

She nodded.

"Of course," Jim Taylor continued, "he's used to being treated with respect—even deference—but that doesn't keep him from being deferential to others who deserve it. You should have seen him out at Rancho Las Flores with Don Fernando Ibarra. He was as polite and respectful to old Don Fernando and Doña María as if he had lived here all his life."

"He is a gentleman," said Doña Alma.

"Well! You are making me curious," laughed Anita. "Why didn't he come to the party if he was invited?"

"He would have come," answered her uncle, "but he doesn't have much time. He is expecting his brother and sister-in-law to arrive next Wednesday, and he wants to have his business taken care of by then so he can show them around, then go back with them to New York."

"It sounds as though he will be too busy to come out to Las Tunas," said Anita. "Poor mother will be terribly disappointed."

CHAPTER TEN

John Vanderburg spent San Juan's Day driving Lolita around El Monte. It was not surprising that he did not care for anything he saw there, since he was prejudiced against it before Lolita ever trotted down the main street. However, he dutifully looked over the area and spent much longer on it than he would have had he not been trying to do his duty. Even then he did not take long.

On his return to Las Tunas he made an extended loop to the northwest and passed through some of the park-like country which he remembered seeing from the train. Huge gnarled oak trees dotted the rolling foothills and cattle grazed there with the great mountains as a backdrop. It was beautiful land, and John appreciated it fully as a tourist, but as a buyer, did not give it much thought. He had been previously informed that it was the property of a man named Baldwin who was not interested in resale.

When Sunday morning came, he found it even harder to pretend to be busy. He had seen El Monte, and Santa Ana was too far to go in a day and return. For awhile at breakfast he toyed with the idea of driving east to a place called Pomona, but he finally admitted to himself that he had no real interest in Pomona or any place other than Las Tunas. Having faced that fact, he was happier, and he finally concluded that the next thing to do was to explore Las Tunas alone and decide which part of it he liked best so he would be prepared to make an intelligent offer to Lawson.

Accordingly, he walked to the livery stable and took out Lolita again. This time, knowing what he wanted, he was very thorough and retraced slowly some of the roads he had followed with Lawson, stopping often to get out of the buggy and look at the soil and plants, and to compare locations with others he had seen.

He traced the edge of the weedy vineyard that Lawson had said belonged to the Aldons and followed it to an equally weedy orange grove which led him to the base of the San Gabriel foothills. He passed a narrow dirt drive leading to a small adobe house shaded by two of the big lacy pepper trees, as Jim Taylor had called them, but he did not stop. He remembered what Taylor had said about the widowed Guadalupe Aldon and her lack of business ability. Besides, he was not sure if she was at home as yet.

Instead he attempted to trace the southern and eastern edge of her property where it touched Lawson's. It was not difficult; he assumed correctly that the well-tended lands belonged to Lawson and that the weedy and ill kempt fields and orchards were part of the Aldon acreage. Only once was he at fault and that was where the boundary passed through an uncultivated section of natural brushland.

By the close of the afternoon he had concluded that the Aldon property was indeed a choice piece of land despite its current lack of upkeep, and that Lawson's deliberate lie about its not being for sale was undoubtedly due to Lawson's own hopes of acquiring it cheaply. He made up his mind that he would make Lawson an offer on the section adjoining the Aldon land on the east which included some fine level fields and some orchards, as well as a large wilderness area running up into the mountains. The two pieces together would make a satisfactory holding.

The more he looked at this land and considered its possibilities, the more he liked it. He sat in his gig looking across a field where cattle were grazing. The late-afternoon sun cast a golden light over animals and vegetation alike, and the mustard flowers growing in the field were an even brighter gold. Behind and above the fields stood the majestic mountains, and the sky over everything was a deep, cloudless blue.

He filled his lungs slowly with the warm, dry air and sat for a few minutes savoring his visions of future harvests. He saw wine being pressed from his vineyards, grain being threshed from his fields, crates of oranges being loaded on to freight cars at his own railroad siding. He saw himself standing on the porch of a house in the foothills looking out over his land—and then beside him he seemed to see a slight, graceful figure and a pair of dark eyes in a laughing face with a dimple.

At that unlikely image, he shook his head sternly and drove back into town to the stable. Still, his plans made him lighthearted and in spite of himself his spirits kept rising as he walked to the hotel. The day had been well spent and was almost over—and tomorrow he was going to see María again.

John was up so early Monday morning that he had to dawdle over his dressing and breakfast. Even after spending what seemed an interminable time in the dining room, it was still early when he finally started out, and he arrived at the bridge over the canal a full fifteen minutes before nine. In a quarter of an hour he expected to see María coming along the same road he had taken from the town, since he believed she lived somewhere on the eastern side of it.

He stood for a time on the bridge, keeping an eye out for her approach and amusing himself by throwing down bits of sticks to float away on the water beneath him. After a while it occurred to him that María had been following the canal when he saw her last, so there was a good possibility that she knew a shortcut to it from her home, wherever that was. So he climbed down to the water level and sat down in the shade of the bridge in such a position that he could watch the path in either direction.

He was looking toward the point where the path disappeared on the east side and was beginning to feel that he had waited a long time, when she suddenly called "Good morning!" from the bridge over his head. He jumped to his feet at once and replied, "Good morning," then reached out to help her clamber down the embankment.

She placed her small hand in his and flashed him a dimpled smile as she slid down to stand beside him. She was wearing a rose colored calico dress with little white flowers printed on it, and today her thick hair cascaded freely down her back. She lifted her eyes to his face as she landed beside him, and the dark beauty of them, as well as the touch of her hand in his and the sudden sweet scent of her, made him catch his breath. She was everything he remembered, and more.

With a conscious effort, he released her hand, but he couldn't take his eyes away from hers, and he stood gazing down into those beautiful depths until shyness seemed to come over her and she looked away.

"I hope you have not been waiting long," she said.

"Not long at all."

"And do you feel like . . . I mean, are you sure you want to take such a long walk and climb?"

"Of course." He smiled at her. "I'm ready whenever you are."

"We can take our time," she went on. "We needn't hurry.

See? I brought a lunch," and she held out a rather lumpy bag she was carrying looped over one arm.

"A picnic?" he asked. "That's great! But isn't it pretty heavy for you?" He reached out his hand to take it from her.

"Oh, no!" she exclaimed. "It's not heavy. It's only a small lunch. I can carry it."

"Nonsense," he said firmly, and, taking the bag from her, he slipped the straps over his shoulder. "There. It's no trouble at all, and I still have both hands free. Shall we go? Lead on."

"All right," she said, "this way," and she started off eastward along the canal.

John's spirits soared as he strode along behind the slim girl and watched her dark hair swinging above her hips as she walked. How free and natural it looked. He had a quick flash of wonder that he, John Claremont Vanderburg, of New York and Newport, should actually be walking this path behind this beautiful creature in this incredible country. And he was going to stay here! The thought came to him again with a pleasant shock. He wouldn't have to leave. This really was going to be his home. He knew now that he would not return to New York with Gordon and Alice when they came; he had too many things to do here to leave so soon. When he did go back east, it would not need to be more than a quick trip to pack up his things and make the final move to California.

The canal began to bend southward, and the girl in front of John made a quick turn in the opposite direction, into the brush, taking a dim trail which John never would have seen. She looked back to see if he was following, and flashed him a smile.

They were angling toward the mountains now, and John saw that a ridge of the foothills jutted out into the valley ahead of them. A quarter of a mile farther on he could definitely see that they were headed for the ridge. In fact he thought he could make out a path climbing up the side of it.

"Is that where we are going?" he called.

She looked to see where he was pointing and nodded. "Yes. We will start climbing up ahead there by those rocks."

A few moments more and the path reached the base of the ridge, wound up through the boulders she had pointed out, and suddenly became a trail clinging to the steep side of the hill and reaching higher as they advanced. John thought the steepness of the trail must be a little hard for María to manage, because she slowed down considerably and kept looking back at him apologetically. He smiled reassuringly to let her know he did not mind the slower pace, and when they had topped the first rise and reached a slightly level stretch, he spoke.

"Perhaps we should sit down for a few minutes and rest a bit."

"Yes, let's," she answered and sat down immediately at the side of the trail.

They were not yet far off the valley floor, but already the view was beginning to open out. Low blue hills were spread across the southern horizon and the roof of the hotel was just barely visible above the cluster of trees that marked the town. Below them to the west was a lemon orchard, which John now recognized as part of the Aldon property. The path they had followed from the canal was plainly visible below, angling across the eastern part of the Aldon land.

"I see where we are now," said John. "You lost me coming through that brush down there."

"We will be able to see much better when we get a little higher," she said. "Do you see that oak tree standing alone up there?" She pointed up the side of the mountain to a natural promontory where a single tree stood out from the low brush surrounding it. "That is where we are going."

"It doesn't look very far," said John.

She giggled—a liquid, musical sound, unlike any John had ever heard.

"It isn't—if you were a bird and could fly straight up. But following the trail takes a little longer."

She was once again sitting on the bare ground with her knees drawn up in front of her, her arms folded across them, as she gazed out over the brushland below. It was the most natural position in the world and she looked quite comfortable, yet John could not think of a single other woman of his acquaintance who would even consider putting herself in such a pose. He knew his sister-in-law, Alice, would stay on her feet until she fainted rather than seat herself on the ground.

A thousand questions came into his mind that he would like to ask her, but they were personal questions, and, therefore, as a gentleman he could not ask them. He sighed.

"Are you rested?" he asked finally. "Shall we go?"

"If you're ready," she said and sprang up as though she had never been tired.

She led off up the trail, and though it was not steep, she did not walk fast but kept a leisurely pace. The trail wound in and out around the sides of hills and ravines and periodically doubled back on itself and climbed at the opposite angle for a while. Despite her healthy appearance, María evidently tired easily, for they rested often, and during one of the pauses John began asking her the names of the flowers he saw here and there on the hillside. He was intrigued that she was never at a loss but readily gave a name to each one, as if they were old friends and she was pleased to introduce them to him.

There was wall flower, and sticky monkey, and lupine, but every so often she would shake her head and say,

"I am sorry; I do not know it in English. It is *echevería,*" or *chicalote* or *espuela del caballero*. "That means 'the spur of the horseman'," she explained after this last.

"Spur?" repeated John. "Oh, of course, it is like our larkspur. There are larkspurs in my mother's garden at home."

"Really? And are they like these?"

"Yes, only bigger. And of course there are whole beds of them, not just one or two plants."

"That must be lovely," she said. "How nice that your mother likes gardening. I wish my mother did."

John had a quick mental image of his mother, in one of her elegant morning gowns, standing on the terrace and giving directions to the head gardener.

"Well," he said, "she doesn't really care much for gardening, but she does love flowers."

"At least she grows them," said María. "My mother cannot be bothered with growing anything. I am the one who does our gardening."

"Do you?" asked John. "What do you grow?"

"Oh, everything. Flowers and vegetables. Vegetables, mostly. I always have a big vegetable garden. You should see my tomatoes and my *chiles*."

"I'd like to."

"Does your mother grow vegetables, too?"

"No," said John. "I'm afraid she isn't interested in vegetables."

"I suppose not. Most people who like flowers don't care about vegetables. I don't know why. I love everything that grows. I think a field of corn all tasseled out is as beautiful as any bed of flowers."

"So do I!" agreed John heartily, "and I think a field of alfalfa is prettier than any lawn."

"Yes!" she laughed, dimpling at him.

He caught his breath again and looked away.

Finally they reached the oak tree that was their goal and sat down together in its grateful shade. John pulled out a handkerchief and mopped his face. María dug into a pocket in her skirt and produced a small square of lace-edged cotton for the same purpose.

"Give me the bag," she said. "I brought some lemonade. We can drink it now and have water with our lunch."

"Lemonade!" exclaimed John. "That *is* a lifesaver."

She loosened the gathered top of the bag and rummaged inside, finally bringing forth a tightly corked bottle and a tin cup. She carefully worked the cork loose, poured the yellow liquid into the cup, and handed it to John.

"It's not very cold," she apologized, "but it's wet."

He drank thirstily from the cup. "It's great," he sighed, and watched María tilt the bottle up to her lips. "Here!" he protested. "You should have given me the bottle and kept the cup for yourself."

"Why?" she asked, taking a breath. "I don't mind drinking out of a bottle."

Tipping the bottle up, she drank again and John found his gaze caught by the smooth golden skin of her delicate throat as she swallowed. He shook his head, amazed again by the wonderful strangeness of this girl. He tried to imagine Alice drinking out of a bottle and could not. He took another sip from his cup and sat gazing out over the valley, now far below and looking very quiet and peaceful in the morning light.

"Isn't it beautiful?" María said after a moment.

"Very beautiful," murmured John.

"I never get tired of looking at it," she confided shyly.

"I can see I'm going to want to climb up here often," admitted John, and he was rewarded by a smile and a grateful look from the beautiful eyes.

"Do you really like it that much?" she asked looking pleased yet wistful. "Of course, it's my home. I've lived here all my life, and I've never seen any other country. But you come from way back east, and I thought maybe . . ." She stopped.

"That I wouldn't appreciate it?" finished John, smiling. "I assure you, it is as beautiful as any place I have ever seen, and I have seen much of the eastern seaboard and the middle west. I've also seen France and England."

She looked up quickly. "You've been to England?"

"Yes. England is very tame and cold compared to this. France—the south of France—is a little like this . . . if it were not so crowded and the people so very different."

"My father was English," she said. "He used to talk about the beautiful gardens there in Hertfordshire, but he said the same thing: that it was cold."

"Your father was English!" exclaimed John. "Why, I thought you were Spanish."

She gave an arch look and an adorable toss of her head. "I am Californian," she said.

"Well, I'm an American," said John, "but I'm also Scotch, English, Dutch, and Algonquin."

She laughed with him then. "If you put it that way," she said, "then I am Spanish and English . . . as well as Californian."

John looked out again over the wide valley stretching away beneath them. "As a matter of fact," he said, "I'm going to apply for adoption."

"What do you mean?"

"As a Californian. Will you adopt me?" he asked lightly.

She did not smile. "You mean . . . ? You're going to stay here?"

"Yes."

Suddenly John also became serious. He wanted her to know how much this really meant to him.

"I've decided to make my home here. For the rest of my life."

She had been looking into his face as he spoke, her great eyes wide and questioning, and suddenly he seemed to see pain there. Then she dropped her lashes and looked down at her hands which were clenched tightly. She made no answer. At last he said, "You don't mind, do you?"

There was an almost imperceptible hesitation; then she flashed him a quick smile and a glance from very bright eyes.

"Why, of course not, I think it's wonderful," she said with a slight tremor in her voice. Then she went on more steadily, "We will be happy to adopt you. We'll make a real *paisano* of you."

"Paisano?"

"Countryman," she said. And she gave him such a frank, utterly captivating smile, so full of genuine comradeship, that he was sure he had been mistaken in thinking her feelings had been somehow hurt.

CHAPTER ELEVEN

Anita was distinctly angry with herself for letting her emotions overwhelm her in such an embarrassing manner. It was inexcusable, she told herself. Mr. Claremont never showed any unhappiness. She must help him to be happy, not remind him of his trouble. It was just that he had taken her so by surprise with that remark about the rest of his life! Of course, he had no idea that she knew how short his life was apt to be. But that was no excuse. She must be on her guard against such emotions in the future.

She redoubled her efforts to be friendly and amusing, and had the satisfaction of seeing that he was responding to her with real pleasure.

It was eleven o'clock before they began their descent and they were halfway down, John Claremont in the lead, when he turned to her and asked, "When are we going to eat this lunch, anyway? I'm getting hungry."

"Well," she replied, "that depends. Do you feel like taking a detour around by a little longer route? If you do, I know a really pretty place where there is a little spring and I thought it would be nice to eat there. But if you'd rather not walk that much farther," she hurried on, "we can eat down at the foot of the trail."

"Need you ask?" he said, grinning at her. "I'm ready to go anywhere you lead."

"You seem to be leading *me* at the moment," she pointed out.

"So I am! Well, we'll remedy that soon enough. Come ahead, and I'll follow." And he stood aside to let her pass down the trail ahead of him.

"Actually, I like it better back here," he said. Before she could ask why, he went on, "Now you be Kit Carson and I'll be Fremont and we'll discover California."

"Discover California!" she protested indignantly, "California was discovered long before Kit Carson!"

"But Fremont didn't discover it until Carson showed it to him," said John. "I'm like Fremont; I'm discovering it right now."

"That's all right then," she giggled. "I don't mind your discovering California. I just don't like being Kit Carson. Now, why can't we be Portolá and Father Serra?"

"I'm very much afraid," John said humbly, "that my education was defective. I don't recall learning anything about either one of them in my history classes."

"Why, you poor benighted foreigner! You really must have some classes in California history before we can adopt you."

"I'm ready anytime," he said cheerfully, "if you'll be my teacher."

"I don't know about that; but I'll give you your first lesson: Don Gaspar de Portolá led the first land expedition into California, and Father Serra came with him and founded the missions."

"I'll try to remember, but you'll have to quiz me later to make sure . . . By the way, when are you going to give me my next music lesson?"

"Music lesson?"

"Yes. I practiced just as you told me to," and he began

whistling "La Golondrina." She listened, smiling, as he went through the tune, and when he had finished, she cried, "You really did practice!"

"I certainly did. I'm sure I must have driven Lolita crazy."

"Lolita?"

"The horse I rented. I practiced while I was driving all around the country. Now you've got to harmonize with me to repay me for studying so hard."

"All right," she said, "you start off."

They whistled the rest of the way down the trail, trying several familiar songs after perfecting "La Golondrina". Anita could not remember ever having so much fun before.

When they reached the low ridge where they had first rested on their way up, Anita turned off the trail and headed toward the east. There was no path here; she was simply following a route which was familiar to her. The *chaparral* was sparse and open, with many clumps of wildflowers adding scattered patches of color. At one place the lupines had covered the ground with a wealth of lovely purple spikes.

"Oh, I must pick some of these," she said and she bent down to gather them. As she was collecting the flowers she was aware of John's gaze fixed upon her for a long moment before he also bent down and picked a dozen or so. These he handed to her when she stood up.

"Thank you," she said and started onward, carrying her bouquet.

When she reached the eastern edge of the ridge, she turned back along it toward the mountain, rounded the head of a small *arroyo,* and passed to another ridge beyond. The second ridge was much broader than the first and more heavily wooded, having a scattering of scrub oaks that grew taller and larger as the hillside sloped down toward the valley. Anita and John had descended it for perhaps half a mile, when they suddenly came out of the brush into a cleared area where a natural group of trees formed a small park-like space on the smooth slope of the hill. A number of wooden crosses stood up in the grass as well as a very few rounded granite markers.

"Why, it's a cemetery," exclaimed John in surprise.

"Yes," said Anita, "but it's not used anymore. There is a new one now, down south of town."

"But this is such a beautiful spot—why did they change it?"

She shrugged.

"Mr. Lawson said it was too far out. We used to think it was worth coming a little farther to have our loved ones in such a beautiful place. But I don't think Mr. Lawson loves anyone, so of course he wouldn't care where they were buried."

She approached a small granite headstone and bent down to place a few of the lupines in front of it. There was a single name carved in the stone: ISABEL. Beneath it was the date 1860, and, below that, the word INFANT.

"One of your family?" asked John.

"My sister. She died just a few hours after birth." Anita moved on to a similar marker. "This is my brother."

The marker read: ALEXANDER, 1865, AGE 3 YEARS.

She placed a few more flowers and moved on to a third, this one inscribed CATALINA, 1865, AGE 8 YEARS.

"This is my sister Catalina. She died of whooping cough at the same time as my brother. And this one," she said, moving on, "is my sister Elizabeth. She was the first-born, but she lived only two years. She died in 1850 of pneumonia."

Anita placed a few more flowers, then gathered the remainder into a neat bunch and walked to the one large stone in the plot, where she laid the lupines gently down on the mound before it.

"This is my father. He was the last person buried here."

John stood looking at the granite, reading the inscription. "Alexander William Aldon. Aldon!" he cried, turning to Anita. "Your father was Alexander Aldon?"

"Yes."

"Then it was your father who used to own Las Tunas?"

"Yes, of course. It was he who made the cemetery here. When the first baby died, my mother could not bear to put her somewhere common or ugly, so my father said he would make the prettiest cemetery in the whole country, and he chose this place and had the priest consecrate the ground."

John Claremont stood staring down at the marker.

"1803 to 1883. Eighty years old. And his property was sold when?"

"The *rancho?* It was never sold! It was stolen! They took it away from us for debt, and the debt was due to all the money my father had spent trying to prove it was his land after the squatters moved in and claimed it belonged to them. Oh, it was all very complicated, and the lawyers could do nothing—except take our money," she added bitterly.

"I didn't realize . . ." said John in a tone of amazement. He appeared stunned, Anita thought, by what she had told him.

She shrugged. "Oh, well, it was a long time ago and we were not the only ones. Many Californians lost their land the same way."

"So when did Lawson take over?"

"In 1881. He got it for practically nothing. That is the only way he ever gets anything. He won't buy anything unless he can get it for nothing."

"I can well believe it," said John, smiling grimly. He

looked at Anita, his eyes full of sympathy. "So your parents even had to give up the cemetery."

"Yes. But my father was glad when Lawson started the new one. He said at least now he could be sure that when Lawson died he wouldn't be buried here with little Alexander and the girls."

"But these others are not all your family?"

"Oh, no. They are people who lived on the *rancho* and worked for my father. Here is poor old Enriqueta Muñoz. She worked for my grandmother Falcón for years and years; then, when my mother married, she came to Las Tunas with her and took care of my sisters as long as she was able. I remember her as a very old lady sitting in the sun on the patio."

She walked down a row of crosses. "Here is my father's tanner, Jose Torres. He died of pneumonia the year before Lawson took over, and here is his wife, Edilia, who died just six months later.

"This one is Alfonso Becerra, a shepherd, and this is Jesus Calderón, a *vaquero,* and this is Carlos Montenegro . . ."

"And who was he?" asked John.

"Oh . . . he was another *vaquero* . . . who died young," she said haltingly, wondering if she had made a mistake bringing John Claremont to this place. She sighed and smiled wistfully. "Never mind the rest. Let's go. This place is sad."

She led John out an old rutted road, overgrown with weeds, which followed the ridge down into the valley, but she turned off the road a short distance beyond the cemetery and worked her way down into the canyon to the west. The floor of the canyon was level and opened out as they advanced until it became a wide, flat area sheltered by the two ridges, and shaded by a group of three huge, spreading sycamores.

"Here we are," said Anita as she led the way to a place at

the base of one of the sycamores where a tiny stream of water welled up from the ground and flowed silently off through the grass. The spot where the water emerged had been cleared and deepened to form a basin edged with rocks and plants. Anita took the bag from John Claremont and settled down on the verge of the spring.

"This place is beautiful," said John. "And someone has put in a lot of work here. Who widened out the basin and put those rocks around? Your father?"

"Well, I began it, but Papá helped me. You see, this has always been a favorite place of mine. I began coming here when I was just a little girl. When my father saw what I was trying to do, he helped me. He showed me how to set the rocks to make a basin, and he carried the biggest ones in for me."

She threw a sidelong glance at John to see if he was really interested, and was gratified to see that he appeared to be thoroughly absorbed and did not seem to have been saddened by her remark about the *vaquero* who died young.

He turned an understanding look upon her. "And then I'd guess you planted all this mint and watercress?"

She blushed with pleasure. "Yes," she admitted, "and the miner's lettuce."

"Miner's lettuce? What's that?"

"It's the one with the funny leaf around its stem—like a little umbrella. And these are tiger lilies that I brought from the canyon, too, but they have already bloomed."

She had opened the lunch bag and laid out a large napkin on the ground. On it she spread several small, paper-wrapped packages as well as the empty lemonade bottle and the tin cup. These last she rinsed and filled with the spring water.

"I hope you like *flautas*. They are the easiest thing to bring on a walk like this," she said, and opening one of the packages, revealed a little pile of the rolled *tortillas* fried to a golden crispness.

"What did you call them?"

"*Flautas*. It means *flutes*—because of the shape. Actually, *flautas* should be thinner—these are nearer to being *tacos*—but I like lots of filling in mine. Help yourself."

John bit into one of the *flautas,* and a pleased expression came over his handsome face.

"That's delicious. What's in it?"

"Carne seca."

"Yes . . . ?"

"Dried meat," laughed Anita.

"But it isn't dry."

"Of course it isn't."

"But you said . . ."

"It starts out dry, but then you add liquid to it."

"It starts out dry?"

"Well, actually it starts out wet, like any meat, but then you dry it."

"Let's see now," said John. "It's wet, but then you dry it, and then you wet it again . . ."

Anita burst into laughter, in which he joined her, his gray eyes crinkling at the corners.

"It does sound silly, doesn't it?" she asked.

"Well, I don't care how it sounds," said John. "It tastes wonderful. May I have another?"

Anita handed him a second *flauta,* then opened the last package.

"Here are some little cakes for dessert," she told him, pleased by his boyish appreciation.

The beauty of the place enfolded them as they sat eating their lunch with the cold water from the spring, and a feeling of comradeship and intimacy grew between them. The huge trees spread twisted branches above them like great white arms, and the shade of the foliage was pierced here and there by golden rays of sunlight.

"I can see why you like to come here," said John. "I believe it's the prettiest place I've ever seen, with the spring, and these trees, and the view out between the hills just like a picture postcard."

Anita gave him a grateful smile. "I hoped you would like it," she said. "It has been my favorite spot ever since I was eight years old when I first discovered it."

"How did you find it? It must be more than two miles from Las Tunas. Surely you did not walk so far alone when you were a child?"

"Oh, no. I rode everywhere."

"Rode?"

"On horseback. I used to have my own pony. She was a little black mare with a white blaze on her nose. Her name was Amistosa."

"And you rode by yourself?"

"Of course. Why not? I was a good rider. I rode from the time I was three years old. And everyone knew me; I was the daughter of the *patrón*."

"Yes. I see," said John.

"I always liked to explore," she went on, "and one day I rode up here. After that I used to come often."

She was silent for a few moments, then went on half playfully, half wistfully, "I used to play house here. I would pretend I was grown up and had a handsome husband and we had built our house right over there, where we could look down the *cañon* from our windows, and the spring and the trees were in our *patio*. I even made my father promise to give me this piece of the *rancho* for a wedding present when I grew up. He promised—but of course that was before we lost all of this."

She threw a glance at John. He was gazing off down the canyon toward the valley, his face serious and full of sympathy.

"Your father must have been a fine man," he said quietly. Then he turned to her with a gentle smile. "And what happened to your horse? What was her name again?"

"Amistosa. Oh, she was sold to Mr. Lawson along with all the other horses on the *rancho,* and he sold her to someone else. I have not seen her for years. She may even be dead, she would be old by now."

A frown appeared between John's eyebrows, and a brightness in his eyes.

"Good Lord!" he murmured. "You poor kid."

The sympathy in his voice and eyes surprised her, yet she was glad to see that he could forget his own trouble for a short time out of concern for her. She looked up into his clear, gray eyes, smiling faintly.

"Well, it *was* hard at first. I loved Amistosa and the big old house, but I was old enough to realize that my poor little losses were nothing compared to those of my father and mother. I was too busy trying to make them forget their troubles to think much of mine."

"And did you succeed?"

"Succeed?"

"In making them forget."

"Not really," she admitted, "but at least I think I convinced my father that *I* was not unhappy, and that made everything a little easier for him."

"And what about your mother?"

Anita sighed. "No, I'm afraid I have not been successful with her at all. I don't think I ever can be. You see, the loss of everything has been so much more humiliating for her than for my father. Before he came to California he had been poor more than once—and rich more than once, but Mamá had never known anything but wealth and luxury and hundreds of people working for her. The hardest thing for him was to see *us* suffer, but the hardest thing for her has been the change in our position."

She paused and looked up at John, seeking his understanding. Reassured by his expression, she added in a low voice, "It is not easy to suddenly find your condition lower than many of those who used to serve you."

"No," he said gravely. "No, of course not."

"So now," she went on, "all Mamá wants is to leave here and to move to Los Angeles, where she will be surrounded by her old friends and relatives and will not be so often reminded of the change in her life."

She gazed sadly toward the valley and thought of the changes that must soon come into her own life: how she would lose these walks in the foothills and the canyons that she loved. If that New York millionaire were to buy their land in the next few weeks, this might even be the last time she would ever come to this spring and sit under these sycamores. Sudden tears came into her eyes, and she knew John Claremont had seen them.

"I'm sorry," she stammered. "Sometimes I . . . can't help . . ."

The words trailed off as she realized he was looking at her with an expression that could only be tenderness. His eyes met hers and he seemed unable to look away.

"Oh, Miss Aldon . . . María . . ." he murmured in a voice filled with yearning. "María . . ." he repeated, and the word was a caress.

Wonder flooded through Anita. Was he going to propose?

He was clearly trying to say he loved her. The wonder was succeeded by a wave of happiness, for she knew she loved him, too. She had felt the powerful magnetism of his person from the very first, but there was more than that. He was the only man she had ever known who shared her interests and who respected her feelings and opinions.

He spoke again. "María, I . . . would you . . ." He paused as a sudden thought seemed to occur to him, and he dropped his gaze from hers.

"Yes?" she murmured breathlessly.

He lifted his eyes again.

"Would you . . . like to split this last little cake with me?"

CHAPTER TWELVE

When John realized he was in love with this girl, he felt no surprise, but a feeling of rightness, of recognition, as though it had been inevitable since that first sight of her in the eucalyptus grove. Her natural beauty had filled him with such wonder that he had been thinking of little else since. But the truth had not crystallized in his mind until he sat with her under the sycamores beside the spring and knew this was the perfect spot for building the home he had dreamed of, and he wanted her in it with him forever and ever, raising a family there, and the two of them growing old together sitting on their porch overlooking the valley.

After that he felt that she belonged to him and he listened to her childhood memories as though he were a part of them, as though he were the one she had been dreaming of when she played house by the spring. As she told him more of her past and revealed to him the extent of her misfortunes, he felt a personal loss, a personal degradation, as though he himself had shared in the ordeal. When he saw the tears in her beautiful eyes, he was almost overwhelmed with the desire to take her in his arms and comfort her, and he actually began to tell her that he loved her and wanted to shield her from any further trouble.

Then he had a sudden, wonderful vision. He would wait

until he had bought this land, and then he would bring her here and lay it at her feet as a gift of his love. It need only be a few weeks before the real estate deal went through, and what were a few weeks out of the rest of their lives? It would be worth the wait to see the happy surprise grow in her eyes when he made it clear to her that she need never leave this place and need never be humiliated again, because he knew he could raise her up to a position higher than that she had left.

The whole idea flashed upon him in seconds and convinced him so thoroughly of its rightness that he quickly changed his proposal of marriage to a commonplace question, not realizing that the girl had been aware of his original intention. He was so filled with excitement that he could hardly wait to put his plan into effect, and he wondered if they would get back to town in time for him to see Lawson that very afternoon. The sooner that was done, the sooner he could return to Los Angeles and see about buying the Aldon acreage.

In the meantime he realized that María was depressed, evidently from recounting her family's misfortunes, and he made an effort to cheer her.

"Perhaps," he said, "you will find a buyer for your place sooner than you think and your mother will be happier again."

"That may be," she replied listlessly. She did not smile, and she began to gather up the remains of their lunch into her bag. By the time she was finished, she had blinked away her tears, and she gave John a tremulous smile.

"What about you?" she asked. "Where in California do you plan to settle?"

"I've been thinking of staying in Las Tunas," he said. "I've enjoyed myself so much here that I hate to leave."

"That would be nice," she answered. "Perhaps we will . . . meet occasionally."

"I was hoping you'd take me on some other walks like this one," he said, "and show me more of the country."

"Of course," she replied. "I will be happy to."

Her face was turned up to his, and the look she gave him was so wistfully sweet that he had all he could do to remain firm in his plans and not embrace her.

Then she turned her glance away and said,

"We had better go now. It is getting late."

She gave a last look around at the sycamores and the spring as though saying a silent farewell, and then she led John down the canyon and out onto the valley floor. A half mile out from the mouth of the canyon they came upon the road from the cemetery and followed it as it angled toward Las Tunas.

After a few minutes more walking the girl stopped and turned to John. "I will leave you here," she said. "The road will take you on into town. I'm going this way." She gestured to a set of wheel tracks leading off through the brush. "It's a shortcut."

"When will I see you again?" asked John.

"I . . . I don't know," she answered shyly. "That is up to you."

"May I come to your house?"

"We have not been introduced properly," she replied, dimpling at him. "I'm afraid my mother would not approve."

"Of course! How thoughtless of me!" exclaimed John, brought abruptly back into the real world. "Never mind," he went on cheerfully, "I'll find someone to do it properly. Until then . . . good-bye."

She gave him her hand. "Good-bye."

She walked swiftly away into the *chaparral* and John made

his way back to the hotel, smiling to himself as he walked and whistling an occasional chorus of "La Golondrina".

Anita did not whistle as she walked home, although she was not exactly unhappy. Her feelings were such a mixture of joy and sorrow that she could not have told which was uppermost.

The happiness she had felt when she realized she loved John Claremont and thought he was about to declare his love, and maybe even propose, was still with her. It had only taken her a moment to understand why he had not finished what he had started. A man in his condition would naturally hesitate to offer himself as husband to any girl. He could not know how gladly she would have accepted, how happy it would make her if she could be near him and care for him in his illness. She knew it would be a few years yet before he would be forced to take to his bed, and why should they not have those years together?

Well, she would just have to let him know—in a modest way, of course—that she would not consider it a sacrifice to be tied to a man who was going—might be going—to die in a few years. And she would never admit that death was inevitable! If consumption could ever be overcome by love and care, she would see that John Claremont overcame it.

Of course, her mother might not approve. In fact, as the thought came to her, she realized that her whole family might disapprove. But that was nothing! She would make them see how much she loved him, what a fine man he was, and how much he needed her. If she could just get him to propose! That was the first challenge. He had said he would find someone to introduce him so that he could call on her properly. If he would really do that, she was sure she could find a way to get him to propose . . . and then she would let him see how she felt, so that he would not back off as he had today. Everything would be all right if he would just do as he had said.

But suppose he should decide to stay away from her so that he would not be tempted? He might think he ought to avoid her for her own sake! It would be just like him; he was such a gentleman, so thoughtful and considerate. And if he decided to stay away, she might never see him again! *¡Ah, Dios!* What a world it was where a girl could not go to the man she loved unless she were introduced! Well, she would not worry about that just yet. He had said he would come. She would wait and see.

As Anita approached her home, she saw Emeterio's wagon standing under the pepper tree in the yard, the old horse waiting patiently, flicking at flies with his tail. Anita murmured a word to him and patted his nose as she walked by.

In the house she was greeted irritably by her mother, who was dressed to go out. "There you are, María Anita! Where have you been?"

"Walking," she replied.

"Walking! Always walking! And with no hat in this hot sun. *¡Dios mío!* You were gone so long I thought you were never coming back! I had lunch without you," she finished accusingly.

"I told Concha I would not be back for lunch," protested Anita. "I took some *flautas* with me and ate by the spring."

"Concha has been gone all morning, too," said her mother. "She went down to see how Juanita Ortiz's little girl is doing. But I told Emeterio to hitch up the horse after lunch because I want to go down to see that new dressmaker, and I'm certainly not going to walk in this heat."

Doña Guadalupe's expression lightened as soon as she

mentioned the dressmaker and her mind filled with thoughts more pleasant than the wayward habits of her daughter.

"Come, Anita, wash your face and put on your bonnet and let us go. I am so anxious to show her the crêpe de Chine that Elena brought me. I am sure she will have some new ideas how to make it up."

"All right," said Anita. "But I will have to put on my corset if we are going down into town."

"Well, this once you may go without it. I am in a hurry, and we are only going to see Mrs. Sanders. Her husband will not be home."

When Anita had washed, smoothed her hair, and put on a small straw bonnet, they went out into the yard.

"Emeterio!" called Doña Guadalupe.

"*¿Lista?*" came Emeterio's voice from the garden.

"Yes, we are ready."

The old man appeared around the corner of the house, gave his hands a hurried scrub at the washstand, then climbed into the wagon and took the reins. As they pulled out from under the shade of the pepper trees, Doña Gualalupe lifted a parasol and opened it, holding it over herself and Anita.

"The sun is so hot. I don't see how you can bear to wander around all day without a hat as you do," she said.

"I like it," replied Anita. "I feel the heat more with a hat than without."

"But so much sun is not good for your skin," said her mother, renewing the old argument. "You are ruining your complexion! You are quite brown already. No wonder the men prefer María! *She* has always protected her skin and you see how lovely and white she is. That Mr. Valenzuela could hardly take his eyes off her. How disappointed he was when Jorge announced her engagement to Mr. Carson. Poor fellow!"

"Don't waste your pity on him, Mamá," said Anita, "I don't imagine he will take long in consoling himself elsewhere."

A gurgle of amusement came from Emeterio.

"That may be," conceded Doña Guadalupe placidly, "but I did not see him consoling himself with *you.*"

Anita's chin lifted. "You may be sure he did not."

"¡Seguro qué no!" muttered Emeterio.

"What is this, Emeterio?" said Anita's mother. "You do not approve of Señor Valenzuela?"

The old man snorted contemptuously.

"That one!" he said forcefully. "*No es caballero*—he is not a gentleman. He has no breeding."

Doña Guadalupe was perplexed. "But he is Silverio's friend," she said.

"Oh, Mamá," put in Anita, "Silverio makes a friend of everyone he meets, no matter who or where."

"If that is true," said Doña Guadalupe doubtfully, "he should not bring them home with him and introduce them to the family."

"No, he should not," agreed Anita, "but Silverio has never had any judgement in such things."

The horse turned into the main street of the town and slowed to a walk. As they passed the hotel, Anita threw a quick glance to see if there were any sign of Mr. Claremont, but the verandah was deserted. They drove on down the block, and at the corner Emeterio turned the horse to the right.

A pale young man, very thin and slightly stooped, came out of the grocery as they passed and, seeing Emeterio, smiled and nodded a greeting.

Emeterio touched his hat. *"Buenas tardes, señor,"* he said.

"Who was that?" murmured Doña Guadalupe as the wagon passed out of earshot.

"Oh, that is Señor Williams. He is the one I told you of, the one who has the bad lungs. He is here for his health, but I don't think his health is improving; he is looking worse than when he came."

Anita stared at Emeterio. "That man who came out of the store? *He* is the one who has tuberculosis?"

"*Sí.* He is the one. Did you not see how thin he is?"

"Yes . . . yes," murmured Anita, her thoughts racing. "He is the *only* sick one at the hotel? There are no others?"

Emeterio gave her a puzzled look. "No," he answered, shaking his head. "There are no others."

"I . . . I thought I heard there were two young men at the hotel."

"Oh, *sí,* there is another one; but he is not sick."

Anita's heart gave a leap. John was not sick! He was not dying! He was healthy. *¡Ah, Dios!* The happiness of it! All the rest of the way to the dressmaker's house the words kept repeating themselves in her mind like a chorus of hallelujahs. He was not dying! He was not sick. And he was coming to see her; he promised he would. He had said he would find someone to introduce him, and then he would come.

But if he was not sick, she thought suddenly, then what had made him stop what he had started to say? She was sure that he was starting to propose, or at least to say he loved her. She could not see any reason for him to stop, but of course he could have many reasons of which she knew nothing. He might be having financial problems, though surely he would know that she was poor already and would not mind being poor with him. Ah, well, he had said he would come; she must wait. The big thing, the important thing, was that he was not dying! She must thank the Holy Virgin for that.

Her thoughts were interrupted by their arrival at the home of Mrs. Sanders, seamstress and wife of the Santa Fe station agent. The house was a modest frame building with the newest of wooden gingerbread trim, painted white and boasting a small lawn in front.

Lawns were new to California, brought by the Americans from the east. Californians grew flowers in their yards, and bushes and vines, sometimes in carefully laid out, intricate beds, but the spaces between the beds were hard-packed earth. This spread of clipped green grass was a pleasant novelty to Anita and her mother.

"You many call for us in half an hour, please, Emeterio," said Doña Guadalupe as she descended from the wagon.

"Sí, señora. Media hora."

They passed up a short gravel walk and mounted to a small porch with a scrollwork railing and carved wooden roof supports. The door was opened by a slim little woman with a thick fluff of light curls over her bright blue eyes.

"Ah! Mrs. Aldon! How are you today? And Miss Aldon, so nice to see you. Do come in."

"Thank you," answered Doña Guadalupe, folding her parasol. "And how are you, Mrs. Sanders?"

"Oh, I'm just fine. Enjoying the beautiful weather."

"Beautiful, yes, but so hot," sighed Doña Guadalupe, taking a chair along with the others.

"Hot? Well, yes, in the sun, but not uncomfortable. In the east, you know, at this time of year it is so humid and sticky! But here it is quite comfortable. Especially when the breeze comes up in the afternoon."

"Yes, the breeze does help."

"I see you have some yardage with you. Did you wish something made up?"

"Yes, if you can help me decide what should be done with

it. My daughter from Santa Barbara brought me this lovely crêpe de Chine. I'd like something stylish for summer. I was hoping you'd have some ideas."

Mrs. Sanders jumped to her feet and went to a corner table, where she took a magazine from the top of a pile.

"The new *Delineator* just came in yesterday's mail and there are some awfully pretty new gowns in it," she said, returning to her chair and pulling it up to the center table. "Let me bring your chair up here, and we'll look through it together."

The seamstress and Doña Guadalupe were soon poring over the illustrations in the *Delineator*. Anita stood and wandered to the window, too full of her new happiness to sit still. The world was so beautiful! John Claremont was not sick! They could have many, many years together instead of the few short ones she had permitted herself to imagine before.

What, after all, had made her believe he was ill? She thought back over their first meeting, remembering each word he had said to her. He had said he was staying at the hotel . . . and then he said he was tired and wanted to rest . . . and she had put the two things together in her own mind and assumed he was the sick young man Emeterio had told her about who must walk for his health. How silly of her! She almost giggled aloud when she recalled how she had climbed the trail so slowly and rested so often because she did not want to tire him.

She thought of him sitting beside her on the mountainside, his clear gray eyes gazing over the valley, his lustrous hair lifting in the breeze, and his strong brown hands clasping his knee. Why, he was the picture of health! How could she have imagined him to be consumptive? Then she remembered Carlos Montenegro dancing in the *patio*. Ah, that was why! Poor Carlos. Yes, but thank God it was not poor John. A mist came over her sight, but she blinked it away and smiled. She need not cry for him any more. He was healthy; he would live for years and years!

Behind her she heard the murmur of her mother's voice and Mrs. Sanders's rejoinders.

". . . very pretty, but too dressy for what I had in mind."

"Here is a plainer style, but very elegant. Your blue crêpe would be just . . ."

He had said he was going to stay in Las Tunas. She wondered where he would live, what he would do. Oh, of course, he was a farmer. He would probably settle on one of Mr. Lawson's subdivisions. Why, if they were married, he could help her take care of her father's orchards and vineyards, and if they could make a profit, then perhaps her mother would not insist on selling! Ah, that was too much to hope, especially if that rich New Yorker decided he wanted the property. If he offered a good price, the land might be sold before Mr. Claremont found a way to be introduced, let alone propose marriage. But maybe that Mr. Vanderburg would never come! Maybe he would find a nice place in Santa Ana! Oh, how she hoped so.

". . . I like it very much, if you are sure the neckline will be becoming to me. I have never worn one like it."

"Oh, my dear, yes! It is the newest thing and perfectly suited to your lovely long throat. We will put lace rosettes on each side . . ."

Anita moved away from the window and wandered around the room, thinking of the strange sensations that had filled her when John Claremont had been near her—how weak she had felt after he helped her down the embankment by the canal and stood looking into her eyes. Moving away from him had been the hardest thing she had ever done, as if his body were a magnet pulling her toward him. And the way he had looked at her! She was sure he felt the same way. Ah, what heaven it would be if he would take her in his arms and pull her against him! Her breath grew short thinking of it.

". . . so that's settled. I'll pick up some lace edging the next time I am in town, and . . ."

Anita picked up a book from the corner table and opened it. *Favorite Poems for the Family* she read on the title page. She flipped through the lavishly illustrated pages wondering if Mr. Claremont liked poetry.

". . . really don't know when to tell you to come for a fitting. I have a couple of other dresses I must finish before starting yours. You don't mind waiting?"

"No, of course not, if you're busy . . ."

Anita sighed. Why hadn't John said what he started to at the spring? Could she have been mistaken? Was she so carried away by her own feelings that she had imagined he might be going to propose? She tried to recall exactly what he had said, how he had looked. She remembered the sympathy in his eyes, his sudden exclamation of her name, then the pause. What had he been thinking?

" making several dresses for Mrs. Swenson. Her husband manages the hotel, you know. She helps him with the bookkeeping . . . a very sweet person."

"Is she? We haven't met."

"Oh, I'm sure you'd like her . . ."

Well, it was no use wondering. The main thing was that John would get someone to introduce them and then call on her in proper form. That must be it. He must have thought she would not like such an unconventional declaration from a man she had not properly met. But then, it was she who had reminded him that they had not been introduced. Oh, her thoughts were such a whirl. All she could be sure of was that she must wait until he came to call.

The dressmaker's voice penetrated her thoughts. ". . . and did you know that one of the guests there is a millionaire?"

"No! Really?"

"Yes. He's a son of W. Stuyvesant Vanderburg, the New York financier."

"Vanderburg? Why, that's the one who's been staying with my sister in Los Angeles."

"You don't mean it! Staying with your sister?"

"Yes. There can't be two with a name like that. He had a letter of introduction to my brother-in-law and was a guest in their house. Anita! Did you hear? That Mr. Vanderburg is at the hotel here in Las Tunas! We heard he wanted to see our property, but we thought he had gone to Santa Ana."

"Well," said Mrs. Sanders, "he's been at the hotel for several days, and Mr. Willetts told Mr. Swenson that he'd been looking at some of Mr. Lawson's land."

"Oh, dear! I do hope he doesn't buy from him instead of us! And after he asked particularly about our place! Anita, has Emeterio returned yet? I think we had better get home in case Mr. Vanderburg comes out to see us. I would so hate to be away when he comes."

Doña Guadalupe completed her arrangements with Mrs. Sanders. She and Anita said their farewells and hurried out to the street where Emeterio was waiting.

When they were settled in the wagon and started on the way home, Anita said hesitantly, "I don't understand, Mamá. If Mr. Vanderburg said he was going to Santa Ana, why did he come here instead? And didn't Uncle Jim say that Don Jorge would be with him when he came?"

"I don't know, Anita. I don't understand it either, but you heard what Mrs. Sanders said. There's no doubt he is here now, and he will surely come to see us before he leaves. We must go home and get ready for him."

"Get ready . . . how?"

"Oh, make sure the house is dusted and neat. And I want you to put up your hair and put on your corset so you will look like a lady."

"Mamá! He's not coming to look at me."

"No, of course not, but you never know. Alma says he is a very handsome young man, and so rich, Anita! A little precaution can't hurt. We'll put some powder on your face so you will not look so brown, and you must make an effort to be modest."

"All right, Mamá," Anita replied faintly.

A very handsome young man? And he had been staying at the hotel for several days?

CHAPTER THIRTEEN

When John arrived back at the hotel, he washed up and changed his clothes, whistling off and on in the process. Then he sat down at the small table in his room and did some careful figuring.

When he was satisfied with his calculations, he took a sheet of stationery with the Vanderburg and Sons letterhead from his suitcase and made out a written offer for one full section of land, 640 acres, specifically that section abutting the San Gabriel mountains and lying just east of the town of Las Tunas; the whole to be paid for at the rate of fifteen dollars an acre for the cultivated portions and eight dollars an acre for those that were unimproved.

He placed this offer in an envelope, which he sealed and addressed to Mr. Jonathan Lawson. Then putting on his coat and hat, he walked down to Lawson's office and left the envelope with Willetts to be delivered to the man in the morning.

"Please see that Lawson gets it first thing when he comes in," John said, "and tell him I'll stop in around ten."

Then he took a leisurely and roundabout way back to the hotel, where he again sat down in his room and wrote a letter to his mother.

He described his trip west on the train, his pleasure in the country, and his determination to settle in Southern California. Once, he began to tell her about María.

"I have met . . ." he wrote, but he paused as he suddenly remembered that he had *not* met María in the socially accepted meaning of the word, and his mother would probably have the same prejudice that María's mother had: She would undoubtedly take a dim view of her son picking up with a strange girl to whom he had not been properly introduced.

"I have met some very friendly and interesting people . . ." he went on.

He told her about staying with the Taylors and about his plans to buy property belonging to Mrs. Taylor's sister.

"I will not be able to come home with Gordon," he wrote, "as I want to complete the purchase of the properties I am considering and make arrangements to have them looked after in my absence, but I will meet you at Newport later in the season. Please give my regards to all our friends there."

After supper he wrote another long letter to Professor Taylor at Amherst.

"I want to tell you how excited I am by the agricultural possibilities here," he wrote. "I would not have believed possible the huge variety of plants I have seen growing. Of course, not all crops grow equally well in the same spot, but many do, and with some judicious purchases of separate parcels of land, I expect to be able to raise almost anything with a minimum of traveling between farms—or *ranchos,* as they call them here."

He went on to give details of the things he had seen as well as his impressions of the Professor's brother and sister-in-law and their home. When that was finished he went out onto the upstairs verandah and sat for an hour smoking a cigar and staring at the dark shapes of the mountains.

And then he allowed himself to dream of María.

* * * * *

In the morning John packed his suitcase, ate a late, leisurely breakfast, and read the previous day's *Los Angeles Tribune*, the current one not yet having arrived in Las Tunas.

At a few minutes to ten he met Lawson in his office and spent almost two hours haggling over the amount of his offer. Lawson wanted twenty dollars an acre for the improved land. This John refused to pay but finally offered sixteen. Lawson insisted that the buildings on the property made it worth more than that.

"The winery is on that section, and some horse barns, and two or three small adobe houses," Lawson insisted.

"I tell you what," suggested John, "let's go out and look at those buildings and see what condition they are in. If they are in good shape, I may adjust my offer."

John had carefully looked over the buildings in question and finally offered Lawson a flat thousand dollars on top of his original offer. Lawson accepted at once, and they drove back to town amicably.

"I'll go right up to Sam Davies's office," said Lawson. "He's our local lawyer, and he can get the papers ready. If you want to meet me there after lunch, they should be ready to sign."

"That's fine," said John. "I want to drive back to Los Angeles later this afternoon and that will work out just right."

"His office is in the brick building over the grocery," Lawson said. "I'll see you there about one-thirty."

Lawson dropped him off at the hotel and drove away.

John went into the dining room, where he ordered fried chicken and mashed potatoes. When he had finished and the Mexican girl with the looped braids brought him his bill, he slipped a silver coin into her hand.

"This is for you," he said, smiling. "I'm checking out this afternoon, and I want to thank you for your excellent service."

"Oh, señor!" she cried. "It has been my pleasure. You come again, no?"

"Perhaps I will," he replied thinking, *Why not? After all, I'll soon be a local resident.*

The girl's eyes followed him as he walked out and then she slipped his coin into the front of her dress before she began to clear his table. John would have been amazed had he known that the coin was never spent, even after she had been married and many times a mother, but lay in a cigar box among other treasures of ribbons, baby hair, and cheap jewelry in an adobe shack on Las Tunas' south side.

The session in the lawyer's office was brief and businesslike. The papers had been drawn up and were pronounced satisfactory by both John and Lawson. The lawyer's secretary was then called in, and also the dentist from across the hall, to witness the signing of the contract of sale.

"Now that you're a member of the Las Tunas community, Mr. Vanderburg," said the lawyer, "I expect we'll be seeing you often."

"Yes, I imagine so," replied John.

"Do you intend to make a home here?"

"Yes. Yes, I do."

Hands were shaken all round, and John left the office, descended the stairs to the street, and went out into the sunlight. He followed the sidewalk as far as it went along the edge of the building, then stepped off into the dirt, and headed toward the back street and the livery stable. He looked at his watch. It was five minutes past two. It took him another half hour to have Lolita harnessed to the gig, settle his stable bill, drive around to the hotel, pick up his suitcase, and check out of his room.

As he drove out of Las Tunas, he calculated that he would arrive in Los Angeles in time for dinner with the Taylors. West of town, he guided Lolita into the ford through the river and found himself whistling "La Golondrina."

Tuesday was a long, tedious day for Anita after an almost unbearable Monday evening. No New York millionaire appeared at the Aldon adobe, but Doña Guadalupe had insisted upon readying herself and Anita in case he should materialize.

The parlor of the little house was dusted and polished until the mahogany of the old furniture glowed. Fresh lace tidies were spread on the backs and arms of the upholstered settee and chairs; lamp chimneys were washed, and the plush cover on the center table was removed and shaken thoroughly outside the back door before being replaced.

Doña Guadalupe herself had donned a plain black silk broadcloth gown, suitable for a genteel widow of refined tastes. Anita's dress was another matter. Much thought and discussion was put into it.

"You must wear something especially becoming and elegant," her mother insisted more than once.

"But you don't want me to look as though I had dressed up especially for him, do you, Mamá?"

"No . . . no. But still . . . I suppose your new green silk is too elaborate. How about your blue one?"

"No, Mamá, that is a party dress, too. I should wear cotton. There is nothing wrong with this dress I have on."

"But you have been wearing it all day and it is not fresh. And besides, you must put on your corset! I would die of shame to have a man like that see my daughter dressed like a

servant with no corset. Especially with a figure like yours, it is so evident! If your bosom were flat, it would not matter as much."

Anita had finally ended the discussion by putting on the corset and a summery dress of white muslin.

Then they had waited.

The waiting was agonizing. Anita had worked on her embroidery while sitting stiffly upright in her corset. And thought. The thoughts were almost as uncomfortable as the corset.

Could Mr. Claremont and this Vanderburg person be one and the same? And, if so, why had he lied to her about his name? And his occupation? He had said he was a farmer! Anita had not heard that Vanderburg wanted to farm the land he was looking for, and she could not imagine that the son of a wealthy man would wish to become a farmer.

As a Californian she was accustomed to thinking of large landowners as a leisured class who stocked their holdings with great numbers of cattle and left the working of them mostly to hired underlings. Even her father's experiments in vineyards and orchards had been only supervisory; the work had been done by employees. And though she had told John that her father was a farmer, she had meant it in the English sense, a gentleman farmer, because that was what his people had been in Hertfordshire, and that was how Don Alejandro Aldon had thought of himself. But Anita was fully aware of the fact that farmers in America were not gentlemen farmers, and when John had told her he was a farmer, she had mentally placed him with the immigrants who had been arriving in Southern California since the sixties in great, heavy wagons loaded with farm implements and with milk cows tied to the tailgates. It was people of this type who had squatted on her father's land, claiming as their own whatever acreage they

had been able to cultivate—thirty to a hundred acres, no more than that. To think of the son of W. Stuyvesant Vanderburg in the same category as those people was ridiculous! Either John was not Vanderburg . . . or he had lied to her.

All Monday evening Anita tortured herself thinking he must have lied to her. As she listened to her mother's constant comments on propriety, she thought it was only too probable that he had lied. If he was the son of a great family, then he was accustomed to the very highest of social circles, mingling with the most well-bred and well-mannered people in the world, and she shuddered to think how she must have appeared to him when he first saw her: sitting on the ground, uncorseted, with naked legs and feet and whistling. He would have assumed she was a servant girl at the very most.

But he liked me, I know he did! she cried to herself.

Yes, well, she knew what her mother's answer to that would be: Men often like to amuse themselves with light women, but it is never more than amusement; they never marry such women; gentlemen only marry ladies. Was that why he had stopped when he had started to propose? Or had she imagined the entire incident, in her conceit? Had he perhaps been about to make a different kind of proposition, and then thought better even of that because she was so far beneath him?

"Alma says he is a perfect gentleman," Doña Guadalupe was saying, "so we must show him that we are genteel people, that we know how to dress and act properly even though we are poor."

Then another thought struck Anita. John had clearly been surprised to discover that she was Alexander Aldon's daughter. Was it because he had expected Don Alejandro's daughter and Doña Alma's niece to be far more ladylike?

But he liked me, her wounded spirit cried again to herself. *I* couldn't *be mistaken; and he wants to see me again. He asked when he could see me again.*

Yes . . . but she had been the one to remind him that they had not been introduced. Perhaps being properly introduced was not what he wanted. He *had* said he hoped she would take him on more long walks. Maybe all he wanted was another surreptitious meeting with an attractive but obviously low-class girl.

No, no! she cried to herself. *He could not be like that. He never tried to take advantage of me! He was such a gentleman!*

Oh, yes, he was a gentleman, but what had she been? Not a lady, according to her mother. No lady would have made a secret appointment with a strange man. It had felt so right at the time, but now it sounded secret, surreptitious, clandestine. Had it really been that way? Had he thought of it that way?

Throughout the long evening she sat stiffly upright in her corset, fighting tears, patiently working her embroidery. When no one had come by nine o'clock, she escaped to her bedroom. There she shed the hateful corset, hung up her muslin dress, and gave herself up to tears.

By Tuesday morning, after a good night's sleep, Anita had recovered her confidence. She washed her face in the bowl on the commode and greeted the day with a smile at herself in the wardrobe mirror.

How could she have been so silly as to think for one moment that her dear John Claremont was that Vanderburg person? She loved John and believed in him; she knew he would not lie to her. Just because she had made a mistake in thinking him tubercular did not mean that everything else had changed. *He* had not said he was sick; that was her own foolish mistake. But he *had* said his name was John Claremont and that he was a farmer. She was ashamed that she had doubted him for even a moment.

Just because he had been staying in the same hotel with Vanderburg, and both were young and good-looking, was no reason for her to get upset last night, thinking her John must be Vanderburg. Probably, if the truth were known, there was no resemblance between the two at all. That Vanderburg person *couldn't* be as handsome as John Claremont; *John* was not just handsome, he was beautiful!

So she patiently listened to her mother's conjectures at breakfast and helped Concha straighten the kitchen preparatory to another day of waiting for Mr. Vanderburg to appear. She resigned herself to letting Concha water the garden while she hooked herself into her corset, pulled on the white muslin dress, and then sat herself down in the parlor to spend the day embroidering dainty pastel flowers on pillowcases.

Vanderburg did not appear, and the day seemed interminable. By evening Doña Guadalupe was sure that he must have bought somebody else's land instead of hers, and she bemoaned her fate endlessly.

"I just don't know how we will manage if we cannot move to Los Angeles. You will never meet any suitable men here! You will be an old maid and poor all your life, and we will both grow old alone in this miserable house, pinching and scraping to exist."

Anita sighed.

Wednesday morning Emeterio made discreet inquiries at the hotel and returned with the news that the rich Señor Vanderburg was no longer there. Carmen Gonzalez, who worked in the dining room, said he had given her a tip before checking out, and she herself had seen him carry his suitcase to his buggy and drive away. Anita put on an old dress and went for a long walk in the *chaparral.*

CHAPTER FOURTEEN

Jim Taylor was sitting on the porch Tuesday evening when John turned in at the gate and headed up the front walk of the house on Fifth Street. He put down his paper and rose to his feet.

"Well! Well!" he cried heartily, "So you're back. Good to see you, boy." He shook hands with the younger man and then turned toward the house, calling, "Alma! Alma, here's Mr. Vanderburg"; then to John he confided, "She said you'd be here, sure, tonight. Got something special cooking for you; don't know what."

"It's good to be here, sir," said John, warming again to the cordiality of these people.

Alma Taylor appeared, smiling, in the doorway. "Mr. Vanderburg! Welcome back. Did you have a good trip?"

"Very good, Mrs. Taylor. I enjoyed every minute of it."

"Come inside. I expect you will want to wash up and have something cool to drink before supper. Your room is just as you left it."

"Thank you, thank you. I'll only be a minute. I just want to wash off some of this dust."

By the time John had deposited his suitcase, washed his face and hands, and brushed the dust of the road from his clothes, Jim Taylor had poured them each a drink and was waiting for him at the foot of the stairs.

"Shall we go out on the porch? It's cooler out there."

John took his drink and followed Taylor outside, dropping gratefully into a rocker.

"¡Salud!" said Taylor, lifting his glass. "And how was Santa Ana?"

"¡Salud!" replied John. "I never got there."

"Never got there! Well, where in hell did you go?"

"I went to San Gabriel first, as I intended. From there I meant to go to El Monte. He paused and took a sip of his drink.

"Well?" said Taylor impatiently. "Where *did* you go?"

"I came to a fork in the road," John reminisced. "One fork went to El Monte, but I took the other one and went to Las Tunas."

"Well! And what then? You surely haven't been there the whole week?"

"Not quite," John admitted ruefully, "but almost. I did go down to El Monte on Saturday, but nothing there interested me, so I went back to Las Tunas. The truth is, Mr. Taylor . . ."

"Call me Jim."

"Thank you, sir . . . Jim. The truth is, I decided right away that Las Tunas was the place I wanted. I spent a lot of time driving—and walking—around there, looking over the land and deciding exactly what I wanted to do. I saw Mrs. Aldon's place—oh, I didn't actually go onto the property, but I went all around it—and I definitely want to make her an offer, if you'll introduce me to the brother who's handling it."

"Of course. That's no problem. He's in town now. We can see him any time. Tomorrow morning, if you like. Or we could walk over after supper, though evening's not the best time to catch him. He often goes downtown after supper for a drink with some of his friends."

"Tomorrow morning will be fine," said John, contentedly savoring his drink and gently moving the rocker back and forth. "My brother's train doesn't get in until around three, so I'll be free until then."

"So you liked Las Tunas, did you? I'm not surprised. I've always thought it was pretty nice myself. I'm not a farmer, of course, so I don't know too much about the agricultural angle, but old Don Alejandro—Alexander Aldon, that is—seemed to do pretty well with his crops. Lawson, the present owner, doesn't farm much. He's only interested in subdivision. Did you meet him while you were there?"

"Yes, I saw him. He took me over his place," said John, wondering if he should confide in Taylor about the land he had already bought. He felt so close to these people that his first instinct was to tell them everything; but he could not say anything about María because he very much wanted to surprise her with his ownership of the spring. He did not want her to learn of it from someone else, and, after all, this man was her uncle. So he decided on a cautious middle course.

"I may buy some land from Lawson," he said carefully. "If I get the Aldon place, it would be nice to have some of the Lawson land adjoining it."

"Well, there shouldn't be any problem about getting Doña Guadalupe's place," Taylor assured him. "She's been wanting to leave there ever since her husband died. She'd have sold out to Lawson, in fact, if Don Jorge hadn't absolutely forbidden it as head of the family."

"Forbidden it!" exclaimed John. "Why?"

"Because Lawson didn't want to *buy* it; he wanted to steal it," said Taylor dryly. "Offered her what it was worth twenty years ago, something like six hundred dollars, if I remember correctly."

"Good Lord!"

"Exactly."

John sipped his drink thoughtfully. "How large a house is on the place?"

"Not large. Four rooms is all. There's another one-room house where a couple of old servants live, and a stable and two or three sheds, I believe. Not much in the way of buildings, but the land is excellent, or so I'm told. Everyone says it's the best in the area."

"Yes," said John. "I think so."

"Well, we'll go see Don Jorge in the morning and find out what he has to say."

A warm glow of contentment surrounded John as he sat rocking and gazing out at the quiet street. He could hear pleasant kitchen sounds coming from the house, with occasional soft, Spanish voices and the clink of china and silver from the dining room. The world seemed very, very good to him at that moment. Everything was proceeding exactly as he wished. Tomorrow he would take the first step toward acquiring the rest of his land . . . his and María's. Her mother could have her money and move to Los Angeles, and he and María could build a place of their own in the canyon by the spring, assuming that she would marry him of course. But he had few doubts on that point.

He was, after all, the son of W. Stuyvesant Vanderburg, with all the advantages of that relationship. He was also aware that María liked him and was as drawn to him as he was to her. That breathtaking moment under the bridge, as well as the lingering glances of her dark eyes, had told him so. If she liked him that much as an ordinary farmer, he had no doubt of winning her as the wealthy John Vanderburg.

Doña Alma's voice called them in to supper, and they rose and followed her into the dining room. They were a happy group as they sat down to eat, and John, reveling in his future prospects, was the most lighthearted of the three. He laughed and talked, telling them of his adventures in the country, omitting mention of María but describing the hotel, its guests, and the untiring activity of the children on the verandah. He told them about the real estate dealer who had tried to sell him a dairy farm, and how he had entertained Lolita with his whistling.

Doña Alma was frankly elated over his decision to buy her sister's land. "She will be so pleased! She has been very unhappy since Don Alejandro died. Now she will come to town to live and perhaps we can help her to be more contented."

It was the most pleasant evening John had spent in a very long time—the exact opposite of the one Anita was enduring with her mother in Las Tunas—and when he retired to bed, he fell asleep with a smile on his face.

Wednesday morning, when John walked down town with Taylor, he left the hardware merchant at the entrance to his store and went on to a barber shop in the next block. The place was crowded, and he read a copy of the *Times* while waiting his turn in the chair. President Cleveland had given a speech in New York in which he called for the lowering of certain tariffs, and the *Times* had quoted him extensively. The Knights of Labor were threatening another strike in Chicago, and the Grand Army of the Republic was demanding an extension of veterans' benefits. But for the most part, John saw, the *Times* showed more concern with the local real estate boom than with national affairs.

So did the barber who cut his hair. A heavyset man with a handlebar mustache, he began plying the scissors and talking at the same time.

"Just out from the east?" he began. And, hardly waiting

for John's affirmative answer, he went on, "Looking for property, I'll bet. Everybody wants in on the boom. Can't say I blame 'em. Between you and me, I've done pretty well myself. In fact, if you're looking for city property, I happen to have a couple of lots for sale right now. Choice location down on Grand. Great for development, if that's your idea, or make you a tidy profit reselling in a month or two, the way things keep goin' up. Not interested? That's all right, somebody else will be. Heh! Heh! Like I say, I've done pretty well. Expect to retire from barberin' before long. If it's country land you're interested in, I've got a jim-dandy piece I picked up out in Burbank at the sale last week. Five-acre plot. No? Well, you're missin' out, I tell you. Better get in the game—there's money to be made! Why, my wife's brother run nine hundred dollars up to nine thousand in just two months, buyin' and sellin', and I've done almost as well."

John left the barber shop smelling of pomade, and returned to the hardware store. He found Taylor and Carson in the back office, immersed in a small sea of papers spread over Taylor's desk.

"Back already?" exclaimed Taylor as John shook hands with Steve Carson. "Look, I'm not going to be able to go with you this morning; we've got a problem here. There's a shipment of goods down at the harbor and some kind of mistake on the bills of lading. I've got to go down to Wilmington to straighten it out."

"I'm sorry to hear it," said John. "Nothing serious, I hope."

"Oh, no, I'm sure we'll get it fixed up, but I'm sorry not to be able to go with you to see Don Jorge. You won't mind going alone?"

"Of course not. Just give me the address, and perhaps a

note of introduction, I'll be on my way."

"Sure thing. Here. I'll write it down for you and also a little note for Don Jorge."

Taylor scribbled a few words on his letterhead and handed it to John, then jotted a street number on a memo pad. "Here. That should do it. You can catch the streetcar out there if you want; it goes within half a block; and that note will introduce you. He's half expecting you already."

John thanked Taylor and walked out the front of the store to the street, nodding at Pedro, the clerk, as he passed. Stepping out onto the sidewalk from the dark interior of the store, he was once more amazed by the brilliance of the California sunlight. It seemed so much brighter here than in other places; the sky was so clear. Even the dust rising from the hooves of the passing teams in the street did not seem to dim the all-pervading radiance.

He glanced up the street and saw a horsecar advancing slowly from the north, so he speeded his steps to the corner, arriving in plenty of time to board the car when it halted in front of him. Once aboard, he paid his fare to the conductor and took a vacant seat behind a Mexican woman with two small children. The open car was not crowded and made few stops as it proceeded sedately on its zigzag course through the residential streets of the city.

At the corner of Fourth and Hill, John got off the car and walked up the east side of Hill, looking for the number Taylor had written for him. Halfway up the block he found it, a large old adobe that obviously predated the newer, frame houses on either side of it. With no yard to speak of, it stood close to the street, only a narrow porch separating it from the roadway. A servant girl was sweeping the adobe paving blocks of the covered area and looked up at him curiously when he stopped in front of the house.

"Does Don Jorge Falcón live here?"

The girl nodded.

"Is he at home?"

Again the girl nodded, then added, "*Sí,* señor, he is here."

She leaned her broom against the house and preceded him through the doorway. The door led into a wide hallway that passed straight through the house and opened onto a patio at the far end. John could see flowers and greenery beyond a deep, shady porch, and from somewhere in the far reaches of the patio he could hear Spanish voices and feminine laughter.

The maid opened a door just ahead of him on his right and glanced into the room there. "You wait in here, *por favor.* I go call him."

Removing his hat, John passed through the doorway as he was bidden and found himself in a small room fitted up as a comfortable study or office. A massive mahogany desk with tall bookshelves above the work surface stood against one wall. The desk was open, and revealed pigeon holes stuffed with papers. A small window near the desk opened on the street side of the house, while another, larger one looked into the *patio.*

John walked to the inner window, hoping to get a better view of the *patio,* but could see only the nearby porch because of a thick bougainvillea vine clinging to a roof support opposite the window. The vine was in bloom and masses of purple blossoms spread out on both sides, effectively blocking the view beyond. The porch itself was empty as far as John could see, which was not far, since the wall was thick and the window deeply inset.

Shortly, however, he heard footsteps, and a man passed the window, heading for the hallway and the door through which John had entered. John turned and faced the door as Don Jorge Falcón stepped into the room.

"Good morning," said the older man in a deep, resonant voice. He spoke and stood with a calm dignity that immediately recalled to John's mind the portrait of this man's father which hung in the parlor of the Taylor home. Don Jorge was not tall, but his firm, upright carriage and proud, uplifted head gave him the effect of height.

"Good morning, sir," said John. "I have a note for you from Mr. James Taylor which will introduce me. I am John Vanderburg." He handed Taylor's note to the other man.

Falcón hardly glanced at the note before tossing it onto the open desk. "Ah, yes, Mr. Vanderburg," he replied, and a faint smile touched his aristocratic face. "I understand you are a guest of Mr. Taylor and my sister."

"That's right, sir. They very kindly took me into their home, and they have treated me as though I were one of the family."

"Naturally," said Don Jorge. "Please sit down."

"Thank you."

Falcón took the chair in front of the desk while John seated himself in an armchair opposite.

"I am interested in buying Mrs. Aldon's property in Las Tunas," began John, "and I understand from Mr. Taylor that you are handling it for her."

"That is correct."

"May I ask if you have set a price on the place?"

Falcón shook his head and spread his hands in a purely Spanish gesture. "Property values in California have been changing so rapidly in the past few years, Mr. Vanderburg, that one cannot set a price on anything. Values change from day to day. Did you have a figure in mind that you wish to offer?"

"I have not seen the place well enough for that," said John. "I've not seen the buildings at all. I would like to make arrangements to drive out there when it is convenient with Mrs. Aldon and look over the property. Until then I couldn't make an intelligent offer."

"That is sensible. Well, let us see. I have a man in my employ who is going to San Bernardino on business for me tomorrow. He can stop by my sister's *rancho* on his way and leave a message that we will be coming, since I will accompany you, of course. When would you wish to drive out?"

"The sooner, the better," said John. "Would Saturday be too soon?"

"No, I believe not. I will be free Saturday."

"Very good. Then I will call for you Saturday morning. Will nine o'clock be convenient?"

"Certainly."

Don Jorge stood up and smiled. "And now, Mr. Vanderburg, would you take a glass of wine with me?"

"I'd be pleased to, sir."

"If you will come with me, I believe my wife is in the next room, and I am sure she would like to make your acquaintance."

John followed his host out and across the hall to a door on the opposite side. This was a wide, double door that now stood open, revealing a large, long parlor, elegantly furnished. A young man about John's age stood beside a heavy table smoking a thin Spanish cigar, and a small, dainty woman sat near him in an armchair so big that it made her look like a child.

Don Jorge put a hand on John's shoulder as they approached the woman. *"Amor mío,"* he said, "let me present Mr. John Vanderburg. My wife, Mr. Vanderburg."

John bowed, and the lady smiled. "I am pleased to meet you, señor."

"It is my pleasure."

"And this is my son," said Don Jorge.

The young man removed the *cigarillo* from his lips and extended a languid hand.

"Enrique Carlos Falcón y Carrillo, at your orders," he recited formally.

John grinned. "John Claremont Vanderburg, at yours," he replied, shaking the limp hand.

"Sit down, please," murmured Señora Falcón. "We have heard nice things about you from Doña Alma."

"That was very kind of Doña Alma," said John. "I'm afraid the truth is that I have been a very poor guest, coming and going at odd hours."

"Mr. Vanderburg is going to take a glass of wine with me," said Don Jorge, opening a cabinet at one side of the room. "Will you take one, Carmelita?"

"A very small one, please."

"And you, Enrique?"

"Of course, Papá."

Don Jorge lifted a decanter and glasses from the cabinet and proceeded to pour.

Enrique settled himself in a chair and gazed at John with frank curiosity. "My uncle Taylor tells me you are a farmer," he said, plainly disbelieving.

"Yes, that's right," replied John. "I studied under your uncle's brother at the Massachusetts Agricultural College."

"Oh, does he teach farming? I knew he was a professor, but I had forgotten what he taught."

"He is an excellent teacher," said John.

"So now you intend to farm in California," said Doña Carmelita.

"Yes, when I have acquired the land."

"All this farming is very strange to us," said Enrique, shaking his head as a sign of his lack of understanding.

"Why is that?" asked John politely.

"There is so little water," said Enrique, "and we have droughts regularly. While I do not wish you any bad luck, I cannot help thinking you would do better to stick to cattle. California has always been good cattle country."

"I am sure you are right," replied John, "and I would not consider farming here without irrigation. Any land that I buy must have a plentiful water supply."

Don Jorge handed a glass of wine to his wife and one to John.

"You must forgive my son," he said. "He speaks entirely from a cattleman's viewpoint. Our family have been cattlemen since the first Falcón arrived in California."

"I expect to raise some cattle in addition to my other ventures," said John. "I believe in diversification. The best way to avoid disasters in any particular business is to have several others going at the same time."

Don Jorge handed a glass to his son and raised his own.

"That is worth a toast," he said. "To your success in many ventures."

"Thank you." John smiled.

CHAPTER FIFTEEN

His short visit with the Falcóns had seemed to John like a glimpse into California's past. He would have liked very much to have seen the rest of the house, particularly that intriguing *patio*, but of course, he could hardly ask. When he stepped back out into the street, he felt as though he were leaving a former era enclosed within those adobe walls, a gracious past that the house jealously guarded against the onrush of the modern world.

He returned uptown and ate his lunch alone at the Elite Cafe. Afterward he went to the Nadeau Hotel to check the reservations he had made earlier for Gordon and Alice. Then he went to the livery stable to secure the use of a larger buggy in place of the gig, which was too small for three people.

When these chores were done, he walked leisurely to the Southern Pacific Depot to await the arrival of the train from San Francisco. He was early and had plenty of time to smoke a cigar and read a copy of the *Atlantic Monthly*, which he purchased at a newsstand in the depot. The articles interested him only slightly, and he found his attention wandering instead to his plans for future crops on his land, improvements he intended to make, and above all, the thought of María waiting for him in their own house.

He envisioned a comfortable, restful home brightened by

her dimpled smile and the sound of her whistling. He laughed to himself at that thought and wondered what his family would think when they found out his wife whistled. And what gossip there would be if news of it ever went beyond the family! He could just imagine Mrs. Astor's cultured voice saying, "My dear, have you heard that John Vanderburg's wife actually *whistles?*" He chuckled aloud. The thought was amusing, but he didn't give a damn what any of them thought.

He got to his feet when the train from San Francisco was announced and strolled out to the platform. Outside, the usual assortment of real estate dealers and promoters were waiting to accost the new arrivals. While the train was pulling in, John saw that there were two sleepers and several day cars. As the brakes squealed and the train came to a stop, he headed toward the Pullmans and stopped in a spot where he could watch the exits of both cars.

When the first passengers descended, they were immediately greeted by a noisy mixture of friends and promoters, and the noise increased as more and more climbed down from the cars to join the crowd. John saw no sign of Gordon at either door and was beginning to wonder if he and Alice had missed the train, when he heard a voice calling behind him.

"John! John, we're over here."

He turned and saw his brother waving to him from beside the last car on the line, beyond the Pullmans. The car had no markings on its sides, so it took John a moment to realize it must be a privately owned car.

Gordon began walking toward him, and they met midway along the length of the car.

John gripped his brother's hand and grinned. "What's all this?" he asked, nodding his head toward the car. "Whom are you traveling with?"

Gordon grinned in response and pounded him on the back. "Why, I'll have you know this is Fenton Collingwood's private car! We're in solid, little brother! Best stroke of business we ever did, to accept that invitation."

John looked incredulous. "You mean to tell me he liked you so well he lent you his own private railway car?"

"Not just us," Gordon admitted. "We're traveling with his younger daughter, Miss Evalyn Collingwood."

"I didn't know there was a Miss Evalyn Collingwood," said John. "I've never seen her."

"You've never seen her because nobody else has either. She's not 'out' yet."

"A schoolgirl?"

"Not any more. She's had two years of finishing school in Paris and was presented last season in San Francisco; but of course that doesn't count in New York, and Mrs. Warren—her older sister, the one we were visiting, you know—isn't satisfied. She wants Miss Evalyn to 'come out' in New York, too. So Alice volunteered to take her as our protégé and have her 'coming out' party at our house."

"That's just like Alice."

"Isn't it?" agreed Gordon. "Well, of course, I didn't object. I could see her old man practically eating out of my hand! So we're taking her east early—or she's taking us, rather—so Alice can begin early fittings for her clothes and other preparations. Mrs. Warren will come along later, in September."

"Well! I'm glad your visit was a success, even if you are saddled with Miss Collingwood."

Gordon grinned again—like a Cheshire cat, John thought. Then he became serious.

"It's not so bad. She's a rather nice girl, really. Awfully young, of course, and inclined to show off her French, which *is* excellent. But see here," he went on, lowering his voice, "she's heard about you and is dying to meet you. Be sure you're nice to her, even if she is a little silly. Now, don't look at me like that! Of course, I know you'll be a gentleman, but be a little *extra* nice, won't you? She's her father's pride and joy, and her opinion of all of us will go a long way toward cementing relations between Vanderburg and Sons and the Collingwood interests."

"All right! All right!" exclaimed John ruefully. "I think I can promise you not to upset the apple cart."

"Great! I knew we could count on you, boy. You're a pretty smooth operator when you're interested enough to bother. Now come on and meet the ladies; and then I'll have to find the station master and make sure he got Collingwood's instructions about parking this rolling palace."

They climbed into the vestibule of the Collingwood car and Gordon opened the door to the interior. At once all resemblance to a railway car ceased. John found himself in a luxurious parlor, thickly carpeted, paneled in polished woods, and hung with heavy velvet drapes. Lamps shaded with cut crystal hung from brackets on the walls, and the chairs were deep and comfortable.

Alice was sitting in one such chair, perfectly poised, dressed in her usual exquisite taste, and looking expectantly toward the door as her husband entered with John. Another chair was occupied by a younger but equally elegant girl in a dark silk traveling dress. She was very slim, almost thin, with honey-colored hair carefully arranged in ringlets and puffs on top of her head.

"Here he is!" cried Gordon. "I finally found him."

Alice stood up and came toward them. "John! How well you look! This climate must agree with you."

She offered him her hand, and he gave her a brotherly kiss on the cheek. "And you're looking lovely, as usual, Alice."

"Thank you. Come and let me introduce you to our new friend and hostess. Miss Collingwood, this is my brother-in-law, John Vanderburg."

Miss Collingwood lifted pale hazel eyes trimmed with dark amber lashes and gazed speculatively up at John. "How do you do, Mr. Vanderburg?" she murmured and extended a dainty hand with polished oval nails.

John took the hand and pressed it gently. *"Enchanté de faire votre connaissance,"* he said.

The hazel eyes opened wide, and rosy lips smiled. *"Ah! Parlez-vous française?"*

"Oui, je parle un petit peu."

"C'est très merveilleux!"

"I really speak very little," admitted John boyishly, "but I had a lot of fun practicing when I was in France, and people seemed to understand me, though I couldn't always understand them."

"But your accent . . . *c'est parfait* . . . really perfect!"

"Merci beaucoup."

"Were you very long in France?"

"A few months is all," replied John, "but I understand you have actually lived there."

"Yes. I was at school there for two years."

"In Paris?"

"Just outside."

"How lucky! I would have liked to attend the Sorbonne, but I was stuck at Harvard, instead."

"*Je ne comprend pas*—I don't understand," said Miss Collingwood. "Why could you not attend the Sorbonne if you wished?"

Gordon gave his deep, booming laugh. "You don't

know our father!" he exclaimed.

Miss Collingwood looked from him to John, questioningly.

"Father thinks foreign travel is fine," explained John, "but for education he insists on American institutions."

"Then he will disapprove of me, *n'est-ce pas?*" said she, with a roguish pout.

"No indeed!" Gordon protested hastily.

"Not at all, my dear," added Alice. "It is only for sons that he has this prejudice. I am sure it would have been different if he had had a daughter. He has never seemed to disapprove of the year I spent in Geneva."

A knock sounded at the entrance to the car, and a Negro servant appeared from a back room to answer it.

"May I speak to Miss Collingwood, please?" asked a voice from the vestibule.

"Yessuh! Step in, suh."

A man wearing the uniform of the railroad appeared in the doorway, his hat in his hand. "Miss Collingwood?"

"I am Miss Collingwood."

"Glad to know you, miss. My name's Burns. I'm in charge of the yards here. We've had orders to leave your car off here until further notice. Is that right, Miss?"

"Yes, Mr. Burns, that's quite right. My friends and I will be sightseeing for a few days."

"All right, Miss. I'll see that you're uncoupled and put on a siding right away."

"Thank you," she replied with a contemptuous look at the official. Then to John she murmured in French, "What a stupid man! How do you suppose he intends to place me there?"

John merely smiled.

Then Alice spoke politely to the railroad man. "Will the

siding be close to the street, Mr. Burns? I would rather not be climbing over a lot of tracks on our way in and out."

"Oh, certainly, ma'am. We have a siding with its own platform at the far end of the yards, where it'll be real private. I hope that'll do."

"I'm sure that will be satisfactory," said Alice with a gracious smile.

"Fine," added Gordon.

"When do you think you'll be leaving?" asked Burns. "We'll need a few hours' notice."

"I'll notify you myself," said Gordon. "I'm Gordon Vanderburg."

"Vanderburg?"

"That's right. I'll see that you're notified in plenty of time. Previous day be all right?"

"Oh, yes, sir. Just fine."

"Very well. Nice to meet you, Burns," Gordon said, escorting the official to the door.

"Well, that's taken care of," said Gordon, returning to the center of the room. "Now, what's next on the agenda?"

"We want to see the town, of course," Alice declared. "Don't we, Evalyn?"

"*Certainement* . . . of course."

"Then I suggest," said John with a smile, "that I get off the car—before Burns starts putting Miss Collingwood on the siding—and go after a buggy. Fortunately, I reserved a two-seated phaeton for sight-seeing before you arrived. I'd have brought it up already if I'd known you weren't going to the hotel."

"That's fine," agreed Gordon. "I'll walk down with you. I haven't had a chance to hear how your land hunt has been progressing."

* * * * *

The two men left the car, walked through the depot, and out to the street.

"Well, what do you think of this country?" began Gordon.

"It's great!" answered John. "I've found the place I want, and I'm working on the deal now."

"No fooling! That's fast work. You *have* been busy."

"It was mostly luck," said John. "The place I'm buying happens to belong to Jim Taylor's sister-in-law."

"Taylor?"

"Professor Taylor's brother."

"Oh, yes. He gave you a letter of introduction, didn't he?"

"That's right."

"What sort of man is the brother? I think you said he owned a small business of some kind—hardware, was it?"

"Hardware, yes, but he's a gentleman and his wife is a real lady. Her family are some of the best people in the area—real aristocrats, make no mistake."

"You'll have to introduce me," said Gordon.

"I intend to. In fact, I promised Doña Alma—that's Mrs. Taylor—that I'd bring you around to call. She apologized for not having room in her house to put you up while you're in town."

Gordon stared at him. "Put us up? In her house?"

"That's where I'm staying."

"The hell you are! And you say she apologized because she didn't have room for me and Alice?"

"Yes."

"I'll be damned."

"They're the most hospitable people I've ever seen," added John. "I did promise you'd all come to dinner some evening while you're here. In fact she wanted us to come *this* evening, but I said we'd better make it some other time because I didn't know what plans you might have made, and I assumed Alice might be tired after traveling all day."

"I'll be damned," said Gordon again. "If that's the case, we'd better plan on calling there first thing, before we do anything else."

"Yes, I think so," agreed John.

"I'll explain to Alice when we get back," Gordon said, then he grinned. "I expect it will be a novel situation for Miss Collingwood. She's a little snob—hasn't learned *noblesse oblige* yet, in spite of her French training."

They walked in silence for a while; then Gordon began again. "This land you're buying . . . is it close to town?"

"About twenty miles east. I'm driving out Saturday morning with the man who handles it—one of the family, by the way. In fact, he's the head of the family. These Californians are as family conscious as our old-line New Englanders. Wait 'til you meet Don Jorge Falcón! He can look down his nose as naturally as any Cabot or Lodge."

"And who is Don Jorge Falcón?"

"He's the man who is showing me the property—the brother of the owner and Mrs. Taylor."

"I see. And you say you're going out Saturday? Maybe I'll come along. The old boy sounds interesting."

When they returned from the stable, Gordon was driving the phaeton behind a pair of handsome bays. They found that the Collingwood car had been moved in their absence to the far end of the yards, where there was a small private platform, as the yardmaster had promised.

The ladies were soon ready, and as Gordon helped them into the buggy, John took up the reins of the team. Gordon climbed up beside John and pulled out his watch.

"It's only four-fifteen," he said. "Have we time for a little turn around town before we call on your friends?"

"Yes, I think so. Taylor doesn't usually arrive home until five."

He started up Alameda toward the center of town, where he proceeded to give them a shorter version of the tour he had taken with Steve Carson. Their impressions were similar to his own earlier ones. Miss Collingwood, especially, exclaimed over the crudity and barbarism of the place, until it became clear to all of them that she was comparing Los Angeles to Paris and London, and that she considered even San Francisco to be almost primitive.

The "mansions" on Fort Street did not impress her any more than the shops of the commercial district; John heard her comment scornfully about *les nouveaux riches* as they drove past Judge Widney's home. On the Plaza she stared at the old Spanish Church of Our Lady, the Queen of the Angels, and the venerable old adobe homes surrounding it, much as she would have looked at the pyramids of Egypt or the Indian pueblos.

John began to be a little uneasy about their visit to the Taylors.

CHAPTER SIXTEEN

When they had completed the circuit of the town, John drove along Fifth Street to the Taylor's little house, which had become so familiar to him. He tied the team to the gatepost and then went to help Miss Collingwood down from the rear seat. Gordon had already handed his wife out and was unlatching the gate. Miss Collingwood was staring at the house when John reached up to assist her.

"Your friends live *here?*" she asked wonderingly.

"Yes, certainly. They are not wealthy people," he replied.

"Oh, I see," she murmured, though it was very clear that she could not comprehend that possibility.

Gordon and Alice had reached the porch and knocked at the open door before John, bringing up the rear with Miss Collingwood, reached the foot of the steps.

Jim Taylor himself appeared in the doorway. "Here already?" he said to John. "You almost beat me. I just walked in the back."

"I hope we've not inconvenienced you, Jim," said John.

"No, no!" Taylor assured them. "Come in."

Alma Taylor stepped through the dining room archway at that moment and joined her husband.

"Mrs. Taylor," began John, "I'd like to introduce my sister-in-law, Mrs. Vanderburg, and her friend, Miss Collingwood."

Alice put out a hand at once, which Doña Alma took, smiling. "I am very happy to meet you," she said, "and you," she added, turning to Miss Collingwood, who had also put out her hand after a moment's hesitation.

"And this is my brother, Gordon," went on John.

"I am charmed, madam," said Gordon with his best smile.

"And this is Mr. Taylor, Alice—and Miss Collingwood; Jim, my brother Gordon," finished John.

They all shook hands.

"We are so pleased to make your acquaintance, Mr. Taylor," Alice said. "John has told us how helpful you have been."

"It has been my pleasure," answered Taylor. "John is a fine young man, and we've enjoyed having him with us."

"Won't you sit down?" added Doña Alma. "I'll have some tea brought in, in just a moment." She retreated through the portieres, and John heard her giving directions in Spanish to the hired girl.

Miss Collingwood sat down on the settee and John took a seat beside her. Alice took the armchair in the corner, while Gordon continued to stand in the center of the room, his attention caught, as John's had been, by the family portraits on the wall.

"Those are my wife's parents," said Taylor. "They were fine people."

"What an interesting face on the man!" exclaimed Gordon. "It is like something by El Greco."

"Yes, isn't it?" Taylor smiled. "The real old Spanish features."

"No longer living, I suppose?"

"Not for some years."

"A pity. I'd certainly like to have met him."

"You will meet his son," put in John. "He is very much like the father."

"Yes, that's true," added Taylor. "Don Jorge does have something of the same manner, and some of the same features."

"The same nose," said John.

"Yes," Taylor agreed, smiling, "very much so."

Gordon took a seat beside the center table and Taylor joined him on the opposite side.

"John has been driving us around your town, Mr. Taylor," said Alice.

"Has he?" Taylor responded. "Well, there's not much to it yet, but we're proud of what there is."

"It's growing," said Gordon, "I can see that. Must be some smart businessmen here."

"Yes. Almost too many, I'm afraid."

Gordon's eyebrows went up. "Afraid!" he exclaimed. "Don't you want it to grow?"

"Well, yes, of course. We must have business, but the way it's happening scares me just a little. It's expanding too rapidly to suit me. This current boom, for example. I'm afraid it could come to an end rather suddenly and leave us in the hole."

"Do you mean locally or nationwide?"

"Well, it could be nationwide, though I'm afraid we could get some pretty bad times here without the rest of the country being affected. And we'd *really* be hit hard if the rest of the country had a depression."

"Like eighty-four," said Gordon.

"Yes," agreed Taylor. "Eighty-four was bad everywhere, but the way things are now, a much smaller slump than that could mean a real depression here."

Doña Alma returned to the room and sat down. "Did you

have a pleasant trip, Mrs. Vanderburg?"

"Yes, very pleasant," answered Alice, "and a very enjoyable visit in San Francisco. We were staying with Miss Collingwood's family there."

Doña Alma turned to the younger girl. "Then you are a Californian, Miss Collingwood?"

"Oh, no," Miss Collingwood denied hastily. "That is, my father has a home in San Francisco, but I was born in the east."

"Well, you need not worry about that," Doña Alma assured her kindly. "As my husband says, our most enthusiastic citizens are those who were born in other places."

"Indeed?" murmured Miss Collingwood.

"I'm sure that's true," agreed Gordon. "At least if John, here, is any example. He hasn't even moved out here yet, but already he's boosting the state like a native."

They all laughed at John's expense, and Taylor added, "Yes, we've got him off to a good start. He's going to make a real Californian." Then, turning to John he asked, "What plans have you made for showing these people around?"

"I haven't really made any plans yet," admitted John. "I've been too busy with my own affairs. I would welcome your suggestions."

Doña Alma spoke up quickly. "You must take them to the mission, of course. It is lovely."

"By all means," agreed her husband. "It's a picturesque old place and very much a part of our history."

"Where is that?" asked Alice.

"In San Gabriel."

"Is it far?"

"Not far," answered John. "We can drive out tomorrow morning."

"Perhaps Mr. and Mrs. Taylor would join us?" suggested Alice. "It would be so much more interesting if someone who knows the history could explain it to us."

"Yes, indeed!" Gordon added heartily. "We'd enjoy having you with us."

Doña Alma looked questioningly at her husband.

"Well . . . let's see," he reflected slowly. "We got that shipping error straightened out today, and I can't recall any other urgent business at the store. I think I might take tomorrow off. How about it, Alma? Shall we go along?"

"I would like that," she smiled. "It has been a long time since I have seen the old church."

Doña Alma's maid came into the room carrying a tea tray, which she set down on the center table.

"*¿Es todo, señora?*" she said to her mistress.

"*Faltamos servilletas,* Rosita."

The girl hastily retreated while Doña Alma began to pour the tea. "Do you take sugar, Mrs. Vanderburg?"

"One spoonful, please."

The maid returned with linen napkins, which she placed beside the tea tray, and then left the room again.

"Let me help you, Alma," said Taylor, standing up and handing the first cup of tea to Alice.

"No sugar for me, please," said Miss Collingwood.

John got to his feet and fetched Miss Collingwood's cup and then his own.

As he sat down again beside her, she gave a gasp of surprise.

"What is it?" asked John.

"Why, it is Sèvres! Old Sèvres china!" she exclaimed, holding up her cup. "And so is yours!" Then, after glancing around the room and at the teapot on the table, she added, "It is a complete set."

"So it is," said Alice, looking at her own cup. "Isn't it beautiful?"

"Thank you," replied Doña Alma. "I've never cared much for it myself. I use it because my mother always did."

Miss Collingwood raised her eyebrows. "Never cared for it!" she repeated. "I'm sure you do not realize what you have! It is exquisite and must be very old."

"Not very old," said Doña Alma.

"But I assure you, it is!" insisted Miss Collingwood. "I have seen this type in Paris, and I was told it was eighty or ninety years old."

Doña Alma smiled again. "Oh, yes, about that," she agreed. "It was my grandmother's." She stood up and went to the whatnot in the corner of the room. "If you like antiques, Miss Collingwood," she went on, "let me show you something that is *really* old."

She lifted a small chest from a shelf and returned with it to the center of the room, where she handed it to Miss Collingwood. It was made of some dark, almost black wood, and covered with intricate carving.

The young girl regarded the box with indifference. "It is an antique, you say? A local product, I suppose?"

"No," said Doña Alma, "though it has been here a long while. It was brought from Spain almost three hundred years ago and came to California by way of Mexico."

"Let me see that!" exclaimed Gordon.

Miss Collingwood passed it to him with a slight blush.

"This is remarkable," Gordon said. "Alice, you must look at this carving."

"According to family tradition, it is a Moorish design," said Doña Alma. "It was made in Andalusia."

Gordon and Alice bent their heads over the small chest and Miss Collingwood sipped her tea while her face slowly resumed its normal color. John pretended not to see her discomfiture and began a conversation with Jim Taylor.

"I've been thinking," he said, "that we might take an excursion to the beach at Santa Monica Friday. Would you advise going on the train, or should we take a buggy and drive down?"

"I think you'll find the train quite comfortable," replied Taylor, "but be sure to return before six. That's when the train stops running. In fact, I think you'd better come back around five. If I'm not mistaken, Alma wants to have you all for dinner Friday evening. Isn't that so, Alma?"

"What is that, Jim?" she asked and turned from replacing the chest on its shelf.

"You want everyone to come to dinner, Friday, don't you?"

"Yes," she agreed, "if it is convenient."

"How nice!" exclaimed Alice. "We will be pleased to join you."

"Yes, indeed," added Gordon. "At what time?"

"Around seven?"

"Fine," said John. "That will give us plenty of time to see Santa Monica. And, by the way, what do we do about lunch? Shall we take a picnic, or is there someplace to eat there?"

"Oh, yes, there's at least one small cafe and a fine hotel with an excellent dining room," Taylor assured them.

"You haven't been there yourself, then, John?" asked Gordon.

"No. I've been too busy looking at farmland to spend time at the beach."

"It is a good thing we arrived, then," chided Alice. "It would never do for you to go back east without having been down to the ocean at least once! How would you explain to all your friends that you had been in California and not seen the Pacific?"

John laughed. "I suppose it *would* seem odd. However, I shall have plenty of time to make up for it. I'm not going east for another month at least."

"Another month!" exclaimed Gordon.

"You're not going to be traveling with us?" asked Alice in surprise.

"No, I'm afraid not."

"There's plenty of room in Father's car," said Miss Collingwood. "Please do not think you would be *de trop*."

"Thank you," smiled John. "I am sure I would not be, and I am very sorry to miss a trip in such pleasant company, but I am just not ready to leave yet. I have a number of arrangements to make here, which will take some time."

"Then we will not be losing you as soon as we thought," said Doña Alma.

"Not quite, though I assure you I do not intend to trespass on your hospitality much longer. I shall want to move out to Las Tunas right away . . . if your sister agrees to sell me her property."

"There is no question about that, I am sure," replied Doña Alma.

"I hope not," said John with a smile. "Do you think it will be possible to hire some workers locally? I shall want to have some cultivating done right away."

"Why, as to that, I am sure there are people in Las Tunas who would be glad of some work—don't you think so, Jim?"

Taylor nodded, and she continued, "Mr. Lawson has been almost the only employer there since my brother-in-law died, and I understand he does not pay very well."

"Did you see Don Jorge this morning?" Taylor asked John.

"Yes, I did. We've arranged to drive out Saturday to see

Mrs. Aldon and look over the buildings."

"I believe I'll go along," Gordon added. "I'm curious to see this place that John is so enthused over."

"I'd like you to see it," said John. "Of course I'll take you if you want to go."

Miss Collingwood threw an indignant glance at Alice. "They are planning to leave us all alone for a whole day!" she cried, then turned to Gordon with a pout. "I didn't think you would be so *désobligeant,* Mr. Vanderburg! Can we not all go?"

"Of course we can," said Alice. "We won't be interfering with your business, will we, John?"

"No, certainly not," said John. "It had simply not occurred to me that you would want to go."

"Nor to me," added Gordon. "My most humble apologies, Miss Collingwood. By all means, let us make it a party."

"We'll have to hire another buggy," said John. "It would be too crowded with all of us and Don Jorge."

"That's no problem," agreed Gordon. "We'll need another one for tomorrow, anyway, since the Taylors will be going with us to see the mission."

"Oh, no," said Taylor, "we'll take our own. My horse needs the exercise."

"All right, then. We'll just reserve one for Saturday. And what time shall we leave tomorrow morning?"

"I'll walk down to the stable about eight-thirty," said John, "and bring the phaeton around to the station by nine. Then we can come back here to meet the Taylors about nine-thirty. Is that all right?"

"Why not meet us at the store?" suggested Taylor. "I'll hitch up our buggy early, and Alma and I will drive down to the hardware, and you can meet us there. It'll be closer, and that'll give me time to check the morning's mail and get Steve squared away in case there's anything he wants to discuss before I leave."

"Your clerk?" asked Gordon.

"My partner," explained Taylor. "Steve Carson. A fine young man with a good head for business. I couldn't ask for a better partner."

"But he is more than that, Jim," protested Doña Alma. "He is more like one of the family, especially now that he is going to marry María."

"Yes, that's true," agreed Taylor.

"María!" exclaimed John. "You say Carson is going to marry . . . ?"

"My niece, María," said Doña Alma, smiling with pleasure.

"Yes," added her husband, also smiling. "He finally did it—got himself engaged. And I can't tell you how pleased we are! As Alma says, Steve's always been more like a younger brother to me than just a partner or a friend and now that he and my niece are going to be married, he'll really be part of the family."

"Well, that *is* fine," said Gordon heartily.

"Yes, indeed," added Alice. "Weddings are always nice, and when it is two people you know and love, that is even nicer."

"Sound business policy, too!" laughed Gordon. "The Vanderburgs have always believed in keeping the business in the family, haven't we, John?"

John's mouth felt strangely dry, and he moistened his lips. "Yes," he said automatically. "Yes."

"Well, this has been a pleasure," said Alice, standing up. "Thank you for the tea and for showing us your beautiful old Spanish chest."

Miss Collingwood also rose and murmured her thanks.

"I'm looking forward to our drive tomorrow," continued Alice as the others came to their feet.

"Yes, indeed."

"Oh, yes."

"Hope it will be a nice day."

"So glad you stopped by."

"See you in the morning."

Taylor put a friendly hand on John's shoulder as he stepped out onto the porch and said, "We'll see you later to-night."

John managed a weak smile. "Yes," he answered.

CHAPTER SEVENTEEN

John could not have said how he lived through Wednesday evening. Only his training saved him: Gentlemen do not display their emotions. A gentleman may be dying, but he behaves like a gentleman until the end. John was miserably aware that he was not dying; he felt more as though he had already died. The life seemed to have gone out of everything; he was no longer interested in what was happening or was going to happen.

As he left the Taylors' house, he held himself rigid and refused to think. He would think when he was alone, but not before. He had planned with Gordon to take the ladies to dinner at the Maison Dorée, which had been pointed out to him as the finest Los Angeles restaurant. Steve Carson had said that it was favored by the local men-about-town.

The thought of Steve Carson made John wince, as he recalled how Carson had blushed when he had said he hadn't "got up the nerve to ask her yet." Apparently Carson's nerve had improved . . . and she had said yes . . . and it was María—John's María—Carson had been talking about!

John resolutely pushed the thought away and forced himself to listen to the comments Gordon was making at the moment. There was nothing to do but carry on with their plan for the evening, and John set his jaw, held his back straight, and doggedly went ahead with it, one foot before the other, one minute at a time.

He tried—tried desperately—to appear no different than usual. He was attentive to Miss Collingwood, murmuring a French phrase from time to time; he laughed at Gordon's stories and commented on the food. But his laughter was thin, his smile weak, and his usual ready wit had deserted him.

As he plodded through the evening, Alice became aware that something was wrong with him. She eyed him speculatively. "What's the matter, John? I don't believe you're feeling well," she said at last.

"I . . . I do have a slight headache," he said.

"I thought so. When we get back to the car, I'll give you a headache powder."

So the evening slowly wore away, and when they had arrived back at the Collingwood car, Alice insisted on giving John a headache powder. He took it obediently and used the excuse to leave early.

Free at last, he drove the team to the stable and then walked toward Fifth Street but halfway there he realized he couldn't face Jim Taylor or Doña Alma, so he turned and walked up Bunker Hill instead. There he found a spot where he could sit down in the dry brown grass and look out over the quiet town.

A few lights still glowed in the commercial district, and music from a cantina near the Plaza reached him faintly, but the only street lamps were near the center of town; the residential area lay dark beneath him except for a few dimly lamplit windows. Beyond the houses, the surrounding fields stretched away indistinctly under the starlight.

He crossed his arms over his updrawn knees, as he had seen María do, and laid his head wearily upon them. Now he could think . . . What had happened?

He had lost María, the only girl he had ever truly loved. In such a short time she had become so important to him that his life was suddenly meaningless, the world an empty place, because he had lost her.

No, that was not right. He had not lost her; he had never had her. Only in his dreams had she belonged to him. He had long prided himself on being a practical man, and yet he had allowed himself to build a great dream castle in the air, with him and María in it, living together happily ever after. And the vision of that castle had become so real to him that it had left him desolate when at last the truth had brought it crashing to the ground. The truth was that she did not love him; she loved another man. Stephen Carson.

Quite evidently she had loved Carson long before he, John Claremont Vanderburg, had come to California. Carson had been trying to build up his nerve to propose on that day of John's arrival. When, then, had he proposed to her? John knew Carson had not been to Las Tunas; he had to have seen her in Los Angeles. Of course! She had come in from Las Tunas to attend the family party that Doña Alma Taylor had told him about. That was where she had gone between the time he had encountered her in the eucalyptus grove and the day they met at the bridge.

He, John, might have gone to that same party. If he had accepted Doña Alma's invitation and stayed in town for the party, he never would have known María except as Carson's fiancée, and he never would have built that castle in the air that had so crushed him by its fall! Instead, he had gone chasing around the country and met a girl—a girl with bare feet, sitting on the ground, whistling—and he could no more forget her than he could make time go backward.

She had actually been engaged when they met the second time. And he had been so complacent, so sure that he, John

Vanderburg, could win any girl he wanted! He had a sudden memory of that moment under the bridge when he had held her hand and looked into her great dark eyes. Oh, God! How could she have looked at him that way when she was already engaged to another man? How could she possibly love anybody but him?

An unbidden thought rose in his mind. *Does she really love Carson? Or could I take her away from him?* But he pushed the thought away. Such a thing was unworthy of a gentleman, of a Vanderburg. Stephen Carson was undoubtedly a fine man; the Taylors thought so, and they had known him for years. John had no reason to believe that Carson would not be good to María, and he could give her a comfortable home in Los Angeles. Somewhere out there on one of those dark streets, she and Carson would live together. That thought seemed to complete the destruction of John's air castle. Now even the last lovely ruins were ground into dust.

But life went on. What was he to do? Tomorrow would come in spite of hell or high water. Tomorrow this shell that covered the wounded soul of John Vanderburg had to drive to San Gabriel and admire the mission. And the day after that, Santa Monica. And the day after that he had to face María again . . . and in company. Put the knife in and twist it!

He groaned aloud. It was too much! Could he not throw off the whole plan and go east again without seeing her? Of course, that would mean explaining to Gordon . . . and traveling with Miss Collingwood. He shuddered mentally. And what would he tell Don Jorge . . . and the Taylors? And what about María herself? If the property were not sold, her mother would have to continue living in Las Tunas, which she evidently hated, and she would keep plaguing María and possibly become dependent on Carson.

No, he had to go on with it for María's sake. Buying her

land was the least he could do, a sort of last gift to the girl he loved. A wedding gift, he thought bitterly. How much he had wanted to buy that land just this morning! Now the purchase seemed unimportant—even repugnant. But he would buy the land for her sake and someday, maybe, he would regain his interest in farming . . . in living. He would have to. His father and brothers were financing him; he couldn't let them down. He had no choice but to go ahead as he himself had planned. He had to carry on, as the British say—stiff upper lip and all. He dropped his head onto his arms again.

John sat a long time on Bunker Hill. Finally, when he thought it was late enough that he would avoid encountering his host or hostess, he walked down to Fifth Street and across to the Taylors'. He could see a night light left burning low in the parlor. He slipped quietly into the house and up the stairs to his room. When at last he lay down in his bed, sleep was a long time in coming.

Anita was relaxed and almost happy after her walk Wednesday afternoon, and the evening was peaceful and quiet. Her mother had given up hearing from Mr. Vanderburg for the time being and was reading a new installment of a serial story in the *Ladies' Home Journal* which had arrived in the day's mail. So Anita was left to herself.

She spent some time before dark in the garden, weeding and watering and even whistling a little, quietly, when she was sure her mother was sitting in the parlor on the opposite side of the house. After darkness fell, she sat for a time in the swing on the little front porch and listened to the crickets. She enjoyed the warm dark of the summer evening and the sounds of busy nocturnal life going on around her.

She had reached a state of patient waiting in regard to John Claremont. She had dismissed all her anguished fears of

Monday night and only infrequently even remembered them. She loved and trusted him and therefore she would be content to wait for him. The knowledge that he was sound and healthy still kindled a thrilling warmth beneath all her thoughts of him; everything else was of lesser importance. She considered again her plan of entering teachers' college in the fall but without the excitement she had felt earlier—before she had met John Claremont. There again, everything was in abeyance while she waited to hear from him. She might go ahead with her plan, and she might not. It would all depend on what he wanted to do . . . or was able to do. She could only wait. But she was not impatient. Her love and her confidence in John surrounded her with a quiet happiness and she did not need to hurry to take the next step . . . whatever it might be.

Thursday, shortly before noon, a rider came into the yard and dismounted. Anita recognized him as the *caporal,* the head *vaquero,* from Don Jorge's ranch. He removed his sombrero politely as Anita stepped out onto the porch.

"*Buenos días, señorita,*" he said, and continued in Spanish. "I bring a message from my *patrón* for the *señora,* your mother."

"Pass inside, please," said Anita, also in Spanish. "I will call the señora."

She found her mother in the bedroom. "José Gutierrez, from Los Encinos, is here, Mamá. He says he has a message for you from Don Jorge."

"Well! What can it be? I hope no one is sick."

She walked into the tiny parlor with no appearance of haste and every inch the great lady.

"*Buenos días, José.* How have you been? I trust your family are all well?"

"*Buenos días, Doña Guadalupe. Sí,* they are all well."

"And Don Jorge?"

"Also. Everyone is well, señora. I do not bring bad news. I am going to San Bernardino for the *patrón* and I only stop on my way to tell you that Don Jorge will come to Las Tunas on Saturday, and that he comes with another señor who wants to buy this place."

"Another señor? Is it Mr. Vanderburg?"

"*Sí, señora,* that is his name—Señor Ven-dair-boorg."

"And they are coming Saturday? That is the day after tomorrow."

"Sí, señora, pasado mañana."

"Well, that is good. We will have plenty of time to prepare. Thank you very much, José," she finished graciously. "And now you are going on to San Bernardino?"

"Sí, señora."

"But you must stop for a short while and rest. It is time for the midday meal. Step into the kitchen. Concha will give you something to eat, and you can continue your journey after you have finished."

Doña Guadalupe took the *vaquero* into the kitchen and saw that he was settled comfortably at the table with meat and *tortillas* and coffee and was gossiping pleasantly with Emeterio. Then she returned to the parlor.

"Mr. Vanderburg is coming at last, Anita!" she exclaimed. "This time he really is coming and we will be able to sell this place."

"I wonder why he did not come before when he was here at the hotel," said Anita.

"Who knows? Perhaps he wanted to wait for Don Jorge to be with him. It does not matter. What matters is that he *is* coming, and finally we will be able to move to Los Angeles!"

"Oh, Mamá, don't be too sure yet. Mr. Vanderburg may

not like our place. Remember, he has not seen it yet."

"Yes, yes, I know, but there is no reason why he should not like it. Alejandro always said this was the best part of the *rancho*. We will hope for the best . . . and perhaps say a prayer or two to the Virgin!"

Thursday morning John arose wearily. He felt like an old man, but he dressed carefully, determined to show no outward sign of his affliction. He had laid out a course and was following it; no one need know what it cost him.

He ate an early breakfast with the Taylors, then walked to the stable and had the team hitched to the phaeton. When he reached the railroad yards and entered the Collingwood car, he chatted with Gordon and drank a cup of coffee prepared by the Negro servant while the ladies finished dressing.

After they left the station and drove down Spring Street to the Acme Hardware, John handed the reins to Gordon while he went inside. He had one agonizing chore to perform and he went at it as though he were about to have a limb amputated. He sought Stephen Carson and found him in the back office with Jim Taylor and Doña Alma.

Carson greeted him with a friendly grin. "Morning, Vanderburg. So you're taking Jim out skylarking again."

"Yes," said John. "He and Mrs. Taylor are helping me entertain my guests."

"Well, it's a beautiful day for it. Hope you enjoy yourselves while I'm slaving away with my nose to the grindstone."

"We'll think of you," said Taylor, grinning. "Not often, but once or twice, anyway."

"Thanks," replied Carson. "I knew you would."

"Well," said John, smiling carefully, "you may be unfortunate today, but I hear that's not always the case. I understand congratulations are in order."

Carson blushed. "Yes," he admitted, "that's right." Then with obvious sincerity, "I'm really a very lucky man." And John, studying him intently, saw a deep glow of happiness appear in Carson's eyes. John held out his hand, swallowed hard, then smiled and said firmly, "You have my very best wishes."

Carson shook hands. "Thank you," he said.

John turned to Taylor, his smile still rigidly in place. "All ready to leave?"

"Yes, I think so. Steve has everything under control, don't you, Steve?"

"Sure, no trouble."

"Come along, then, Alma. Let's not hold up the party."

After that ordeal, the rest of the day was merely miserable. John discussed business and agriculture with Gordon; at least that did not require smiling. His ideas about farming had always been a serious business with him, and it was perfectly natural that he was still serious in talking about them. It was a relief to explain his plans for irrigating, cultivating, pruning, fertilizing, hiring labor, and so forth, and he went on about them at great length.

In the back seat, Alice and Miss Collingwood discussed plans for the "coming out" in the fall. They were both animated in their talk of gowns and dressmakers, catering and decorations, and Miss Collingwood plainly reveled in the society gossip Alice casually interposed.

When the occasion arose, John dutifully made it a point to flirt mildly with Miss Collingwood, though her constant French affectations irritated him. Just yesterday he had found them mildly amusing. When they reached San Gabriel and descended from the buggy, he took his place beside her and tucked her dainty, tapered hand into his arm. A sigh of weariness escaped him as he did so, and to cover up, he hastily threw her a weak smile. She mistook the smile for a sign that he was falling in love with her, and lowered her eyes so he would not see the triumph there.

She had her own dreams of captivating the youngest son of the famous Vanderburgs during her first season "out", and becoming queen of New York society. That afternoon she thought she had almost achieved her goal. As a result, she became even more friendly to Alice, and more condescending to the Taylors. As Mrs. John Vanderburg she would see to it that her husband did not consort with such insignificant people in the future.

Doña Alma was oblivious to Miss Collingwood's snubs,and readily answered Gordon or Alice when they directed their eager questions to her. She related the history of the missions and the mission Fathers in vivid words conjuring up the romance of the period in unforgettable pictures for her listeners. Miss Collingwood was only half pretending to listen, but the Vanderburgs were raptly attentive. Occasionally Jim Taylor put in a word or two, but mostly he was satisfied to leave the storytelling to his wife. When Doña Alma mentioned Portolá and Father Serra, John's lips tightened and his eyes stared off over her shoulders.

"Poor, benighted foreigner," he said softly.

"Yes, weren't they?" said Miss Collingwood, tossing her blonde head. Then lowering her voice to an intimate whisper, she added, "And much overrated, *n'est-ce pas?*"

Her words did not penetrate. John heard only the tone.

"Yes, *certainement,*" he murmured automatically.

Miss Collingwood gave him her sweetest smile and squeezed his arm lightly. The effort was wasted. John was seeing a slim girl in a rose-colored calico dress with her dark hair blowing in the breeze.

Friday was a repetition of Thursday, except that in place of the buggy ride to San Gabriel, they had a train ride to Santa Monica, and instead of strolling through the cloisters of an old, weathered church, they walked along the beach and watched the waves run up the sand. The Taylors were not with them today, and John endured an unbroken companionship with Miss Collingwood, who was happily discussing New York and the coming season, with no vulgar California history to interfere.

Once, after lunch at the hotel, when the ladies had gone to the retiring room, John said desperately to Gordon, "For God's sake, stick close to us! Don't let her get me off alone, or I'm apt to forget I'm a gentleman."

Gordon took his cigar from his mouth and gave John a sharp glance. "That bad, eh?" he said. "Yes, I can see you're looking somewhat strained." Then, after another penetrating look at John's face, he suggested, "Come on into the saloon and I'll buy you a drink. The girls won't be back for a while, and you look as though you need something."

He led John into the hotel bar off the lobby and ordered drinks for them both. When they were settled at a table and the drinks had been brought, he regarded John sympathetically and said, "I don't need to tell you how much I appreciate this, little brother. You know as well as I do what it means to Vanderburg and Sons."

John took a lifesaving swallow from his glass and sighed. "Glad I can help," he said tiredly.

"I admit I didn't think it would be this bad," went on Gordon. "I thought she was a pretty decent kid. Meeting the Taylors seems to have brought out her worst."

"That's true," said John, peering into the amber liquid in his glass. "Thank God for that."

"What do you mean?"

"Just what you said. The worst is out. She can't get any worse, can she?"

Gordon grinned.

"Maybe not," he conceded; "but don't forget that repetition makes anything *seem* worse."

John groaned.

"Never mind," said Gordon, serious again. "Only one more day."

"What do you mean, 'one more day'?"

"I mean one more day. We're pulling out Sunday."

"So soon? I was expecting you to stay a week at least."

"I know you were. So was I. But I can't do that to you. You're my little brother, after all. If we were alone, as we'd planned, Alice and I would love to stay. But as it is . . ." he shrugged. "Another time, maybe."

"I don't know what to say."

"Say 'Thanks.' "

"Thanks."

"You're welcome."

Of one accord, each lifted his glass, touched rims with the other, and drank.

CHAPTER EIGHTEEN

Anita rose from her bed reluctantly on Saturday morning. She was not looking forward to the day's events, but it would be good to get it over with and know, once and for all, whether they would have to leave Las Tunas. She was afraid that she already knew the answer, but her fear was not as heavy as it would have been had she not been half expecting John Claremont to take her away from her home, anyway.

If only Mr. Vanderburg could have waited a little longer! Or if only Mr. Claremont had come sooner! Her mother might have been talked into leasing the land to John instead of selling it to Vanderburg. But it was too late now.

Anita hooked herself into her corset, brushed her hair, and arranged it atop her head. Then she took the white dress out of the wardrobe and put it on.

Surveying herself in the mirror, she giggled. "Well, I certainly do look ladylike."

She elevated her chin, smiled demurely and held out a hand to her image in the mirror for an imaginary handshake. "How do you do, Mr. Vanderburg? So nice to meet you! Do please pay us lots of money for our place. It is so very difficult to be genteel when one has no money."

Doña Guadalupe put her head in at the door. "What did you say, Anita? Were you speaking to me?"

Anita laughed. "No, Mamá. I was pretending I was speaking to Mr. Vanderburg."

"Pretending? How silly you are!" And her mother disappeared.

When Anita emerged from her room, she found Doña Guadalupe fussing about the parlor, smoothing doilies and straightening magazines, in spite of the fact that everything in the room had been thoroughly cleaned the day before. She went into the kitchen and poured herself a cup of coffee from the big black pot on the back of the stove.

"*Buenos días,* Concha. Are you ready for the big day?"

Concha snorted. "For the whole week I have been ready! The house is so clean, a cockroach would starve in it!"

Anita giggled.

"I believe you."

"Will you have eggs for breakfast, *mi hijita?*"

"Please. Has Mamá eaten?"

"*Sí.* She arose at the same hour as Emeterio. They ate together."

"Poor Mamá! I don't suppose she slept well, she is so excited."

Concha nodded. "That is the way with Doña Guadalupe. She is always nervous. True ladies always are."

"Really, Concha? Then I *know* I will never be a lady. I am not nervous at all."

"No matter, *mi hijita,*" answered the cook imperturbably, "you can pretend. Wring your hands once in a while and weep a little, and no one will ever know."

"Oh, Concha!" cried Anita, choking on her coffee. "You are so funny! Don't say things like that when I am trying to be a lady. You will make me spill my coffee on my dress."

The old woman grinned affectionately at Anita as she broke eggs into the frying pan and poured *salsa* over them.

"How about you, Concha *mía?*" went on Anita. "How will you and Emeterio like moving to Los Angeles?"

The cook shrugged again. "*¿Que importa?* What does it matter? We have friends everywhere, and one *cocina* is just like another. But truthfully," she admitted, turning the eggs out onto a plate, "I think Emeterio will be very content when he has seen the last of old Lawson."

"Do you think he can find work in Los Angeles?"

"*¿Como no?* Why not? He works well."

After breakfast Concha absolutely refused to let Anita clean up the kitchen, even wearing an apron.

"*¡María Anita!*" she gasped. "What do you think to do? You will not wash dishes in that dress! Go, I tell you. Go and sit down and work on your embroidery."

"All right, I will go." said Anita, giving way. "But," she muttered darkly, "I will be . . . cursed . . . if I will work on that infernal embroidery!"

Concha shook her head, chuckling silently as Anita left the kitchen.

In the parlor Doña Guadalupe was sitting sedately in an armchair with her tatting in her hands. Anita sat on the opposite side of the center table and, sighing, took up the *Ladies' Home Journal.*

Lunchtime came and went with Doña Guadalupe worrying whether they should wait for the guests before sitting down to the meal. Concha, however, insisted that they eat, saying that Don Jorge knew when mealtime was and could arrive at the right hour if he chose.

"And anyway," she finished, "I have some meat I can heat for them if they are hungry."

Doña Guadalupe was still doubtful, but she ate—hurriedly—and returned to the parlor.

It was one o'clock when wheels were at last heard in the driveway, and Emeterio, on the front porch, called in the window, "They come, señora." He stepped down leisurely into the drive to take charge of the horses.

A two-wheeled gig was in the lead, and looking from the parlor window, Anita saw Don Jorge descend first with a dignified greeting for Emeterio, and then . . . *¡Santa Madre!* . . . it was John, her John Claremont, whom she saw stepping down beside Don Jorge! She had barely absorbed the actuality of his presence when she realized that another buggy was pulling up, driven by a third man, a large, imposing fellow, and sitting behind him were two young women—beautiful women in elegant, expensive gowns frothy with laces and ribbons. The big man was Mr. Vanderburg, of course, but why was Mr. Claremont riding with Don Jorge? And who were the ladies?

She watched as Mr. Vanderburg got down from the buggy and turned to assist the elder of the ladies. Don Jorge and John Claremont both stepped over to offer help to the younger girl, who ignored Don Jorge and took John's hand with a smile. Anita understood the meaning of that smile at once and suddenly felt very plain in her white muslin dress. She straightened her back and lifted her chin, but she made no move to accompany her mother as Doña Guadalupe stepped into the doorway to welcome the guests. Instead, she stood waiting beside the table in the center of the room, outwardly calm, but her thoughts in a turmoil.

"Good afternoon, Jorge," said her mother. "How is Carmelita? And the family?"

"All are well, 'Lupe," replied Don Jorge, embracing his sister. "And you?"

"As you see me—in good health."

Don Jorge stepped aside to let the others enter the room and began performing introductions. Anita tried to keep her eyes away from John while her quick glance took in the others, but after a moment or two she realized that he was trying not to look at her, either. She heard the name "Mrs. Vanderburg" with surprise; she thought Uncle Jim had said Vanderburg was unmarried. "Miss Collingwood" came next, then "my niece, Miss Aldon," and at once all eyes turned to her.

"How do you do," she said formally.

Both ladies smiled, but only the older one put any warmth into it. Mrs. Vanderburg put out her hand to Anita and said, "So glad to meet you, Miss Aldon."

Anita grasped the soft, beautiful hand and became aware, for the first time in her life, how darkly tanned her own skin was.

Don Jorge continued with the introductions, and Anita heard "Mr. Gordon Vanderburg." Then, at last, the moment arrived that she had been waiting for with an inexplicable dread.

". . . and Mr. John Vanderburg," said her uncle.

John . . . *Vanderburg!* Anita's eyes widened as all her previous fears came thronging back and coalesced into a painful knot in the pit of her stomach. He was looking into her face, but he was not smiling, and for a moment she thought she saw a reflection of her own hurt in his eyes.

"John Claremont Vanderburg, at your service," he said. He had placed a slight emphasis on his middle name, and she understood he was trying to tell her that he had not lied about that, at least. But she did not offer her hand and she did not smile, and he turned quickly away from her.

"Would you like some coffee or tea?" her mother was saying. "Or can I have Concha fix you something to eat?"

"Thank you, no," Don Jorge replied. "We have already eaten."

"And it's much too hot for tea!" exclaimed Miss Collingwood, taking a fan from her reticule and waving it daintily at herself.

"Then perhaps you would like some lemonade?" Doña Guadalupe offered politely.

"No, thank you, just a little water, please—if you have some that's cold," the blond girl replied.

"Of course. Concha?" Doña Guadalupe spoke without raising her voice.

"*Sí, señora.* I bring it," replied the servant from the kitchen.

When they were all seated, Mrs. Vanderburg directed a smile to Doña Guadalupe. "We stopped at the hotel in the village," she said, "and had lunch. It is a very nice hotel. In fact, I rather wish our visit could be longer so we could stay a few days here. They told us at the hotel that excursions up into the mountains are available from here."

"Yes," answered Doña Guadalupe, "there is a very pretty resort back in the *cañón,* and a stage goes up every other day."

"Perhaps we might come back next year," said Mrs. Vanderburg. "Do you think so, Gordon?"

"I'm sure we could," replied the big man heartily.

"We've enjoyed ourselves so much," went on Mrs. Vanderburg. "We had dinner last evening with Mr. and Mrs. Taylor—your sister, I believe?"

"Yes."

"Very fine people," said John.

"Certainly are," added his brother.

"And Mrs. Taylor gave us a simply wonderful tour of the San Gabriel Mission. It was perfectly delightful! I never had any idea California history was so interesting."

"The missions were very beautiful in their day," said Don Jorge, "and very extensive."

"Yes," Anita's mother agreed, "but it is a shame they are so neglected now. San Gabriel is not so bad, but many of the others are in ruins."

Mrs. Vanderburg nodded. "So Mrs. Taylor told us. Of course, San Gabriel is the only mission we have seen. I would love to see them all, but of course that would be impossible on a short visit."

"But not if we spend the winter here," said her husband.

"Spend the winter, Gordon? Do you think we might?"

"I don't see why not. Didn't we spend a winter in Italy a few years ago? We can just as well come to California, especially after John is settled out here."

"Of course! I keeping forgetting that John is going to live here."

Miss Collingwood stopped fanning herself and looked at John in surprise. "Surely you're not really going to live here?" she said. "I understood you intended to hire someone to manage your property."

"I have no . . . definite plans," said John. "You forget that Mrs. Aldon has not yet been consulted." He turned to Doña Guadalupe and smiled for the first time. "You have a fine piece of land here, Mrs. Aldon, and if you would consider selling it, I would like to make you an offer."

Doña Guadalupe smiled graciously back at John. "I am quite willing to sell," she assured him, "if my brother approves. I have no longer any pleasure in staying here since my husband died. But Don Jorge manages all my business affairs now . . ." *As though it were an empire,* thought Anita, as her mother went on, ". . . so you will have to come to an agreement with him. I am always guided by his judgement." And she gave a nod and smile to Don Jorge as though she were a queen and he her prime minister.

Don Jorge replied with an equally dignified nod of acknowledgment.

Anita felt a surge of pride in these two; this was her family! *I must not disgrace them,* she thought.

Concha came into the room carrying a tray of glasses filled with water, which she began offering to the guests.

"Then, with your permission," John continued, "I would like to take a walk around outside to look at the outbuildings."

"Certainly," replied Doña Guadalupe. "I will call Emeterio. He can show you whatever you wish to see."

"I will call him, señora," said Concha.

"Thank you, Concha."

Miss Collingwood took a sip of water and began fanning herself again.

"Oh, it is so stuffy in here! I believe I'll go outside with you and get a little fresh air," she said, and she let her eyes smile at John over the top of her fan.

He did not reply immediately, and Mr. Gordon Vanderburg spoke instead. "Good idea!" he cried. "Alice, perhaps Mrs. Aldon would not mind taking you and Miss Collingwood for a little walk through that pretty flower garden I saw outside. I'm sure you ladies don't want to tramp through stables and outbuildings with John and me."

"We certainly don't," said Mrs. Vanderburg.

Miss Collingwood looked down and said nothing.

"My daughter will be happy to show you her garden," said Doña Guadalupe. "I will stay inside with Don Jorge . . . unless you are going with the other men, Jorge?"

"No, I think not. Emeterio can show them what is to be seen."

Mrs. Vanderburg turned to Anita. "The garden is yours, then, Miss Aldon?"

"Yes," said Anita, rising, "it is mine. I will show it to you, if you like."

She walked to the door as the other women stood up to follow her, and as she pushed open the screen, she saw Emeterio approaching from around the corner.

"Here is Emeterio, Mamá," she said, then turned to the old man. "The gentlemen wish to look around. Please assist them."

She led the two ladies to the garden and entered by an archway covered with bougainvillea in full bloom.

"How lovely!" exclaimed Mrs. Vanderburg, as she followed Anita along a path between beds overflowing with flowers. Each bed was edged neatly with rocks and contained an attractive assortment of low-growing flowers and taller bushes. Sometimes a small tree stood in the center. The smooth dirt paths between the beds were completely free of weeds and stones and branched invitingly into different nooks and corners, some open and sunny, some shady and cool. The garden was closed in on one side by the house, which was covered almost entirely by climbing roses, past their prime, but still blooming. On the opposite side, a hedge of oleanders separated the garden from the orange grove. In one corner a low bench was shaded by crepe myrtle trees covered in pink bloom.

"Surely you have not done all this by yourself?" said Mrs. Vanderburg. "It must have taken years."

"Yes, of course," agreed Anita. "But I began it when we first moved here—when I was twelve years old. Some of the roses and trees were already here, and as you can see, the flowers are mostly perennials. It takes very little work now."

"Why don't you plant grass along the paths?" asked Miss Collingwood.

"That is not the Spanish way," answered Anita with a shrug. "And anyway, grass *does* take work. I prefer to put in my work on the kitchen garden."

Miss Collingwood lifted her eyebrows. "Kitchen garden?"

"Yes, certainly. I grow vegetables as well as flowers."

"Indeed," said Miss Collingwood.

"Do you really?" said Mrs. Vanderburg. "You must have a very green thumb to grow all this and vegetables, too."

"Would you care to see my tomatoes?" asked Anita with a twinkle in her eye.

"I'd love to," said Mrs. Vanderburg, smiling.

"Oh . . . certainly," added Miss Collingwood.

Anita led them through a gate in a fence overgrown with honeysuckle. Here they saw the same neat beds and bare paths, but the beds were filled with onions and garlic, carrots and peppers. Beyond the peppers were the tomato vines, tied to tall stakes and loaded with fruit, some already ripening, and beyond those was a long section of corn, taller than Anita and rustling in the beginning breeze.

"This is marvelous," said Mrs. Vanderburg.

Miss Collingwood tilted up her nose. "I can understand flowers," she said, "but surely you don't *enjoy* growing vegetables."

"Yes, I do," answered Anita.

"But isn't it awfully dirty work?"

Anita glanced at the other girl's dainty white hands and perfect oval nails.

"Actually," she said, "I like getting my hands in the dirt. It's nice and cool . . . and usually has lots of worms in it."

Mrs. Vanderburg began to laugh. "*Touché,* Evalyn!" she exclaimed. Then, as she saw the expression on the younger girl's face, she added gently, "Oh, my dear, don't be so serious. Miss Aldon was only joking with you."

Miss Collingwood stared at Anita as though she were one of the worms in the dirt.

"Joking! Really!" she said, then to her friend, added, *"Très mauvais goût!"* and turned away.

Mrs. Vanderburg caught sight of a patch of flowers blooming near the onions.

"Some of your flowers seem to have strayed out of place, or do you deliberately mix the flowers with the vegetables?"

"Only when they are edible," Anita smiled. "That is *cilantro*."

"*Cilantro?* I don't recognize the name."

"It is an herb used for seasoning."

"Oh, I see. Isn't it odd that we never expect edible things to have beautiful flowers?"

"Many times they don't, but some do," said Anita. She led the way to a patch of squash plants, where bees were crawling in and out of the open blossoms. "I don't believe there are any prettier flowers than these."

"You are right," agreed Mrs. Vanderburg. "In Italy I have eaten a dish that the Italians make by frying blossoms like these in batter."

"Really?"

"Yes. I forget what it is called, but it is delicious, and they decorate it with fresh blossoms. It makes a lovely, light breakfast, and a beautiful one as well."

"I'd like to try it," said Anita, moving on down the path. "Here are some more of my favorites, even though they are so common." She pointed to a patch of lush greenery where there was a profusion of dainty lavender flowers with bright golden centers.

"*Are* they common?"

"Don't you recognize them?"

"No, I don't. Are they something that I should know?"

Anita giggled. "You eat them almost every day."

"Not these lovely little flowers! They must bear some sort of fruit, but I can't imagine what it might be."

"They are potato blossoms."

"No! Really?" said Mrs. Vanderburg delightedly. "I'd never have guessed!" She bent down over the plants. "May I pick one?"

"Certainly."

"You know, I could make a corsage of these and wear it at one of Mrs. Astor's balls, and eveyone would think it was some exotic hothouse bloom."

"Oh, Alice!" cried Miss Collingwood. "What a ridiculous idea!"

"And what would you say when people asked you what it was?" asked Anita.

"I'd look up the Latin name and give them that."

"*Quelle bêtise,*" said Miss Collingwood.

They strolled back into the flower garden where Miss Collingwood sat down on the bench under the crepe myrtle and fanned herself. Mrs. Vanderburg wandered around among the flower beds exclaiming over the different varieties and asking names of those she did not know.

After a while they heard the voices of the men returning from their tour of inspection and Miss Collingwood got quickly to her feet.

"Shall we go in now?" she said. "I believe I'd like another glass of water."

CHAPTER NINETEEN

The two Vanderburg men were standing in the shade of the porch with Don Jorge and Doña Guadalupe when Anita escorted her lady guests around to the front.

Mrs. Vanderburg approached her husband and held out her potato blossom. "Look, Gordon," she said, "I have a *boutonnière* for you." And she slipped the flower into the buttonhole on his lapel.

He looked down approvingly. "Very pretty," he said.

"And very rare," she told him.

"Then it was very nice of Miss Aldon to give it to you. Thank you, Miss Aldon."

"You're very welcome," said Anita, smiling.

"Aren't you going to ask me what it is?" urged his wife.

"Wouldn't mean anything to me if I did," replied Vanderburg. "You know I don't know one flower from another, especially rare ones. Ask John; he's studied botany along with his agriculture. He might recognize it."

"I wonder if he does." And she looked at John, who was watching with a half smile on his lips but saying nothing.

"Well, what about it?" asked his brother. "Can you tell me the name of Miss Aldon's rare flower?"

John looked at Anita and seemed to smile in spite of himself.

"Alice might have said it was rare, but I don't believe Miss Aldon did." Then, turning back to his brother, "It looks very much like a potato blossom to me."

"Potato! No fooling!" And Gordon Vanderburg gave a great shout of infectious laughter.

"You'd never have known," said Mrs. Vanderburg, "if John hadn't told you."

"No; you certainly could have fooled *me,* but you couldn't put something like that over on a farmer." And he laughed again.

Anita looked at John wonderingly. "*Are* you a farmer?" she asked.

He looked surprised. "Yes," he replied. "I thought you knew."

She lowered her eyes. "I . . . thought I must be mistaken."

"I have a degree from the Massachusetts Agricultural College."

Relief flooded her. He had not lied after all, though she did not yet understand how he *could* be a real farmer. She looked into his face again and would have smiled, but he quickly turned his eyes away from her and spoke to her mother.

"This is a very pretty place you have," he said.

"Yes, I suppose so," replied Doña Guadalupe sadly. "My husband loved it, but for me there are too many memories."

"I understand how you feel," said John, and the sympathy in his voice was real.

"If you have finished your inspection," she went on, "let us sit down here on the porch. Jorge and I have brought out some chairs, and it will be more pleasant than inside."

"Oh, yes, much more pleasant," said Miss Collingwood.

They all chose seats, and Anita found that John had taken the chair beside her, with Miss Collingwood on his other side.

Doña Guadalupe and Don Jorge were facing them, and Mr. and Mrs. Vanderburg were sharing the swing.

"Concha is making some lemonade," said Doña Guadalupe. "She will bring it out in just a moment."

"We certainly enjoyed your daughter's garden," said Mrs. Vanderburg. "She has a real talent for making things grow."

"Yes, she enjoys it. She is like her father; Alexander also had a talent for such things. She does not get it from me."

"Of course, I think your climate must have something to do with it," continued Mrs. Vanderburg. "I have seen an amazing number of beautiful gardens since we have been in California." And she went on to tell Doña Guadalupe about various gardens she had seen in San Francisco and elsewhere.

After they had been talking a few minutes, John turned to Anita and spoke in a low voice. "I have been staying with your aunt and uncle," he said.

"Yes," replied Anita. "I heard."

"And I have met Mr. Carson . . ." he went on, then paused.

"Have you?" she said.

"He . . . seems to be a fine person."

"Yes, he is," said Anita.

She saw his jaw clench, and he began to say something more, but his brother interrupted, calling, "Isn't that right, John?"

"I'm sorry, I didn't hear you," said John. "I was speaking to Miss Aldon."

"We were just saying that Florida's climate is quite different from this. It's much more humid and tropical."

"Yes, that's right," said John.

Concha appeared in the doorway with the lemonade, and Doña Guadalupe said to Anita, "Why don't you bring out some of those little cakes you made yesterday? And also some crackers and cheese."

"All right. I'll get them."

She rose and went into the kitchen. There she got out the cakes and crackers and arranged them neatly on her mother's best plates. When she had finished, she returned to the porch. Mr. Gordon Vanderburg was discussing politics with Don Jorge, and Miss Collingwood was talking animatedly to John.

". . . you have not met my sister yet," she was saying. "I know you will adore her! She has that . . . *je ne sais quoi . . . très charmante . . . comme chère Alice. Ils se ressemblent beaucoup.*"

She was leaning toward John and looking up at him from under her amber lashes when she caught sight of Anita offering a plate of little cakes. She smiled self-consciously and said, "Do please excuse my speaking in French. I have been living in Paris and have become so accustomed to the language that the words just slip out."

"I understand perfectly," said Anita politely. "My mother and I have the same problem."

Miss Collingwood's eyes widened.

"The same . . . ?"

"And I hope *you* will forgive *us* for any Spanish we may have used," Anita went on, knowing fully that none *had* been used. Even Concha had spoken in English.

"Oh, Spanish!" said Miss Collingwood.

"Yes," Anita continued, "we have spoken Spanish all our lives, and of course *you* understand, when a language is second nature, how very difficult it is to avoid being impolite unintentionally. I'm sure you will forgive us."

"Yes . . . of course," said Miss Collingwood doubtfully.

John's brother choked on his lemonade.

"Oh, Gordon! You always drink too fast," said Mrs. Vanderburg, pounding his back ineffectually.

He took a handkerchief from his pocket and buried his face in it, coughing violently.

"Oh, I'm so sorry!" exclaimed Doña Guadalupe. "Can I do anything?"

"No thank you," said his wife. "He'll be all right in a moment, I'm sure."

The head behind the handkerchief nodded, and a smothered voice said, "Sorry. Please excuse me."

After another few coughs he emerged from behind the handkerchief, very red in the face and looking sheepish.

Mrs. Vanderburg resumed her conversation with Doña Guadalupe, and after a moment or two her husband joined in with Don Jorge. John sat silently between Anita and Miss Collingwood.

After about half an hour Don Jorge suggested they should be leaving. They all stood, and the Vanderburgs began expressing their pleasure in the visit, while Doña Guadalupe protested how much she had enjoyed entertaining them.

Anita began collecting the empty glasses, and John said, "Let me help you, Miss Aldon."

He picked up his own glass and Miss Collingwood's and followed Anita into the house and out to the kitchen, carrying the two glasses. Anita smiled at him as they deposited the glassware on the kitchen table where Concha was working, but nothing was said. Then she led the way back into the parlor and was heading for the porch when he stopped her, saying urgently, "Miss Aldon, please . . . just a moment."

Anita turned to face him. He spoke hurriedly and in a low voice.

"I haven't had a chance to thank you for everything," he said earnestly. "For taking me up the trail, and the picnic, and . . . everything. It was very kind of you . . . especially under the circumstances."

"The circumstances?"

"Yes. And of course," he went on, "I realize now it would be better—for both of us—if we didn't meet . . . alone . . . again."

Anita stared at him and her heart contracted painfully.

He continued, "But I had to see you alone long enough to tell you that you have my very best wishes for your happiness . . . always. I couldn't say it in front of the others."

Shock held Anita speechless. He was wishing her happiness, but he was not going to see her again!

He put out a hand as though to touch her but jerked it away again. He tried to smile, but it never reached his eyes, and then he turned away from her and went out onto the porch.

Anita stood still, unable to move for a long, horrible moment. Then she heard Mrs. Vanderburg's voice saying, "Where is Miss Aldon? We must thank her for showing us the garden."

Anita forced herself to walk to the door. She faced the group with a mechanical smile, accepted their thanks, and said her farewells. Her mother was smiling and giving John her hand.

"I will be in touch with you, Mrs. Aldon," he was saying. "Don Jorge and I will settle everything on our way back to town."

"I am looking forward to seeing you again," she said. "Good-bye. Good-bye, Jorge."

John turned once more to Anita as Don Jorge was embracing Doña Guadalupe. He tipped his hat and bowed. "Good-bye, Miss Aldon," he said with a smile as mechanical as hers, then turned away and offered his arm to Miss Collingwood. He walked toward the buggy with the dainty blonde clinging to his side and smiling up at him.

He was out of earshot when Don Jorge embraced his niece and said, "Good-by, Anita, take care of your mother."

She waited until her uncle had stepped off the porch, then turned blindly and ran into her room and shut the door.

Doña Guadalupe stood alone on the porch to wave at the departing guests.

In her room her face wet with tears, Anita knew she had only a few minutes before Doña Guadalupe would come to look for her.

She would have liked to bury her face in her mother's shoulder and cry, "Oh, Mamá, he doesn't love me!" but how could she explain what had happened? She would have to confess that she had met a strange man secretly and had fallen in love with him, that she had behaved as no lady should, and now that he had turned out to be the wealthy Mr. Vanderburg, he had rejected her! Doña Guadalupe would be humiliated beyond words—she who had suffered so much humiliation already.

No, no! She must never let her mother find out the awful truth. But what could she say? She could not stop her tears. How could she explain them?

She quickly moistened a cloth with water from the pitcher on her washstand and held it to her face.

A few minutes later, when Doña Guadalupe put her head in at the door, Anita was lying on the bed with the wet cloth over her eyes.

"They have gone," her mother said, and her voice sounded happier than Anita had heard it for a long time. Then she asked, "What is the matter, Anita *mía?*"

"Oh, I have a *terrible* headache, Mamá! I couldn't wait any longer to lie down."

"Why, that is too bad! It must be from the nervous strain. But no one would ever have known you were nervous. You carried yourself beautifully. I was so proud of you! Can I bring you anything?"

"No, nothing, thank you. I just need to rest. Let me try to sleep."

"All right, dear."

Doña Guadalupe shut the door quietly and went out to the kitchen to discuss the happy events of the day with Concha, while Anita muffled her sobs in her pillow.

She had saved her mother from humiliation, but there was no saving herself. She had let John think she was a shameless hussy—meeting him alone and allowing him to call her by her Christian name, and then letting him know she was willing to meet him again! And he had wanted to see her—or at least she had thought so—but he had changed his mind. Why? "I realize now it would be better for both of us if we didn't meet . . . alone . . . again." *¡Ah, Dios!* Could she ever forget those words? But what did he mean, "now"? What had changed his mind?

Was it because his better nature had told him he shouldn't compromise her? Or had he decided she was too far beneath him even for a clandestine affair? She had a sudden memory of Mrs. Vanderburg and Miss Collingwood—so dainty, so elegant; then she saw herself as *she* must have seemed to him—coarse and dark and plain, with her brown skin and her cotton dresses. Ah, that was why! He had seen that she could not begin to compare with the women of his own class.

If only she had listened to her mother and Concha and kept her skin white, like María. If only she had not agreed to meet him alone. If only he had never seen her barefoot and without a corset—and whistling! If only . . . if only!

The thought of Miss Collingwood hanging on his arm was

particularly galling, because Anita sensed that beneath her beautiful exterior polish, the blond girl was a distinctly second-rate person. Yet *she* had walked beside John as though she belonged there, while Anita was not to be allowed even to meet him secretly for walks in the *chaparral!*

How could she have thought he wanted to propose to her? She had been so sure . . . and so happy! It had been such a wonderful dream when she had imagined John, a poor farmer, and herself, his wife, living together on a little place in Las Tunas.

That dream was all gone now. Her John, whom she loved so, was not a poor farmer but a millionaire's son who preferred Miss Collingwood to Anita Aldon. It was just as her mother had told her. Gentlemen did not want girls with brown skin and work-worn hands. What was it she had said to Doña Guadalupe just before San Juan's Day? "If that is the case, then I will not marry."

And she had meant it! She had not known that in such a short time she would give anything in the world to be fair and blond and clinging to John's arm . . . to be taken into his embrace and held against his body . . . to be kissed by him, his beautiful mouth on hers . . . to belong to him and be his wife. She had not known, but now she knew—would always know, would not be able to forget. She had thought with pleasure of being a teacher. Now she would have to be a teacher, but the pleasure would be gone because she loved a man she could not have.

Maybe in twenty years or so she would be able to smile and say, "Oh, yes, I loved a man once." But, *Ah, Dios!* How long that twenty years was going to be!

When suppertime came Anita told her mother she could not eat. Her head still throbbed, she said, and she was going to bed. The suffering was real, but it was not a headache. It was pure heartache.

CHAPTER TWENTY

The next day was Sunday, and John heaved a great sigh of relief as he watched the Collingwood private railway car pulling out of the station at the end of a line of plebeian Pullmans and day coaches. He had survived Saturday, though he wasn't sure how; it was all somewhat blurred in his memory.

He remembered María, of course—not the dimpled, laughing girl of their earlier meetings, but a dignified, queenly woman in a dainty white gown. He remembered her face when he had mentioned Steve Carson, the quiet smile that had wrenched his heart, and her calm certainty of Carson's good character. He had tried then, out of the depths of his own misery, to wish her happiness, but Gordon had interrupted before he could get the words out.

He also remembered Doña Guadalupe; she had seemed to him like royalty in exile. When he had looked into her aging but still beautiful, unhappy face, he had been glad that he had not abandoned his intention of buying her land. At least he could give her a little pleasure.

Of those moments alone with María in the parlor, he remembered only the awful urgency, the desperate fear that they would be interrupted before he could say what he had to say. He remembered pouring out the words while trying not to touch her, but he did not have a clear recollection of what he had actually said. He had wanted to let her know how very much their meetings had meant to him so that she would understand why he could no longer bear to be alone with her now that she was promised to someone else; and he had wanted to tell her that he sincerely hoped she would be happy in her marriage to Carson, because her happiness meant more to him than anything in the world. Well, he could only hope that he had succeeded.

The drive back to Los Angeles was clearer to him. He had been alone in the gig with Don Jorge, which was a mercy. Don Jorge was a quiet, restful man, not given to levity. They had discussed the property sale and come to an agreement very quickly.

Don Jorge would contact his attorney the following week, and when it was convenient for all parties, they would drive again to Las Tunas for the signing of the papers. Don Jorge was in no hurry and saw no reason why anyone else should be. He had told John that he was going out to his ranch for a few days but that he would see the lawyer as soon as he returned.

After that was settled, they had maintained a somewhat desultory conversation, mostly about the country and its people. At Don Jorge's instigation they had returned to Los Angeles by way of the Rancho Santa Anita and the town of Pasadena, where they had stopped for dinner at the Hotel Greene.

Dinner had been a trial. Everyone but John had been quite gay; a bottle of champagne had been drunk, and even Don Jorge had loosened up enough to toast the ladies in flowery Spanish-style phrases. John had simply endured.

When they had arrived back in town and dropped off the ladies and Don Jorge, they had taken the horses to the stable, and afterward John and Gordon had had a few minutes quiet talk together walking back to the railroad yards. Gordon had enjoyed the day immensely and reviewed its events with enthusiasm.

"I think that's a great place you're getting, little brother. Beautiful country! Almost makes me jealous."

"You can always come to visit," John had said.

"Don't think we won't! Alice is just as crazy about it as I am. You get yourself a comfortable house built, with plenty of room for visitors, and we'll be around, don't you worry."

They had walked in silence for a while; then Gordon had said, "It's a pity the Aldons are moving to town when you take over the place. It would be great to have them as neighbors. What a looker that girl is! And smart, too. I'll never forget how she squelched Miss Collingwood—and the Collingwood never even knew she was squelched!"

"You almost gave it away, though," John had said.

"I did, didn't I? I tell you I wanted to shout! That put-down was so smooth and neat. There's not a dowager in little old New York could have done it any better! If I were you, I'd give that girl a rush."

"She's engaged to Taylor's partner."

"Oh, is she the one? Well, he's a lucky man."

Sunday morning Gordon and Alice and Miss Collingwood had made a farewell call on the Taylors, after which John had gone down with them to the station and spent their last couple of hours together in the private car discussing future plans and possible meetings in various places. Miss Collingwood had been on her most charming behavior, and John had tried very hard to be charming in return. He had felt like a third-rate actor on a second-class stage.

Finally the ordeal had come to an end. All the proprieties had been duly observed, the car had been coupled to the overland train, Gordon had given John's hand a final grip, John had waved . . . and then they were gone, and it was all over.

★ ★ ★ ★ ★

Now he had to decide what to do with himself next. He left the station and went out to the street, walking slowly.

He knew what he wanted to do. He wanted to get out into the country somewhere and be alone for a long time. But where could he go? He kept thinking of the foothills above Las Tunas, but he didn't dare go there; the chance of meeting María was too great.

Nevertheless, the mountains seemed to call him. They had attracted him ever since he had first seen them, and now he had the feeling that if he could only find a way up into them they would somehow soothe his wounded spirit and he could find peace.

It would be easy enough to go out to Las Tunas. He had told the Taylors that he expected to move out there as soon as the sale of the property was completed. It was near enough to completion now that no one would be surprised if he made the move from the Taylors' home to the Las Tunas Hotel. When he got there, he could at least sit on the verandah and *look* at the mountains. If only he could get up into one of those canyons and hide for a week!

Then he remembered Doña Guadalupe had said there was a resort up there somewhere, and hadn't she said there was a stage going up regularly? It was exactly what he needed. He would leave word with Don Jorge that he would be back to the hotel in a week.

He quickened his pace. If he hurried, he could be packed and moved out this afternoon so that he would not have to eat supper with Jim Taylor and Doña Alma, pretending to be happy when he was miserable.

Taylor was in his favorite chair on the porch reading a book when John turned in at the gate. He looked up and greeted the younger man. "I see the train must have got off on time."

"Yes, right on time."

"Too bad your brother couldn't stay longer."

"He'd have liked to," said John, "but he'll be back. Now that he's seen California, he'll want to come."

Taylor chuckled. "That's always the way. I just wish I could get *my* brother out here once."

There was a pause. Then John said, "I'm going to pack up my things today, Jim. I'm going to move out to Las Tunas now that everything is arranged."

"Eager to get to work, are you?" Taylor asked, grinning.

"Well . . . yes," lied John.

"Don't blame you a bit, but I know Alma will try to get you to stay over, at least one more night. She'll want to fix something special for your last dinner with us."

"Where is she?" asked John. "I'll try to explain to her."

"She's around somewhere. Upstairs, I guess."

John went into the house and looked into the dining room. It was empty, and there were no sounds coming from the kitchen, so he went upstairs.

As he approached his room, he saw that the door was open and was therefore not surprised to see his hostess on her knees before an open chest in one corner. A pile of old clothing was on the floor beside her and she was lifting out other articles, adding to the stack.

"Oh, Mr. Vanderburg!" she said, smiling at him. "I hope you will forgive me for coming into your room in your absence."

"Of course," said John. "Can I help you?"

"No, thank you. I am just looking for a certain old dress. I know it is in here, but I must have packed it farther down than I thought."

She continued digging into the chest while John lifted one of his suitcases onto the bed.

"Ah! Here it is!" she cried in satisfaction, and she pulled a bulky folded gown from the bottom of the chest. Clutching her find against her bosom, she was struggling to get to her feet when John grasped her arm and helped her up.

"Thank you," she said. "I am really a little too plump to be getting down on my knees."

"Shall I put the other things back for you?" asked John.

"Oh, no, I will do it in a moment, but first let me show you what I have here."

She laid the heavy garment on the bed next to John's suitcase and unfolded it carefully, disclosing an old-fashioned gown of white silk trimmed lavishly with delicate French lace at the neck and sleeves.

"It is my mother's wedding dress," she told him, smoothing the silk of the dress affectionately. "And this is her *mantilla.*" She spread out a huge shawl of lace as fine as cobwebs.

"It's very beautiful," said John.

"I promised María I would take it to her this afternoon," Doña Alma confided. "She wants to be married in it, and of course it may have to be altered to fit her."

John stepped back as though he had been struck.

"But I must hurry," she added, turning back to pick up the piles of clothing and replace them in the chest. "It is getting late, and if I don't get over there soon, I won't be back in time to put the chicken on for dinner."

John strove to control himself. "She is in town, then?" he said.

"Oh, yes. She has been in town since San Juan's Day. She has never liked living on the *rancho;* so you can be sure she is always in town when her father is."

"Her father!"

"And, of course," went on Doña Alma, laughing, "she has had another reason for coming to town since Mr. Carson began his courting. Why Mr. Vanderburg! Is something wrong?"

John stared at her, unable to move. She moved to stand in front of him, looking up into his stricken face with worried eyes. "Are you ill?" she asked.

Suddenly he put out his hands and took hold of her shoulders.

"Mrs. Taylor! . . . Please! . . . Tell me who it is . . . who is getting married . . . to Mr. Carson."

"Why, my niece, María—María Falcón," she said, wonderingly.

"Falcón! Not Aldon?"

"Aldon? Why, whatever gave you that idea?"

"You said it was your niece, María . . ." he whispered brokenly, "and I thought . . ."

"That it was María Anita? No, no! It is María Concepción. You should have asked."

John sat on the bed, knocking his suitcase onto the floor, and put his face in his hands.

"I . . . never thought . . . you would have . . . two nieces . . . named María!"

"I have *three,*" she said simply. "It is a very common name in California. My own name is María Alma. I was named for my mother, and so were my nieces, for that matter. But I had no idea," she added pityingly, "that it had such importance for you. Please forgive me if I have caused you pain." And she patted his shoulder with her small, plump hand.

John lifted his tear-wet face to look directly and unashamedly at the sympathetic little woman beside him. "It's all right now . . . Doña Alma," and he smiled. "May I call you Doña Alma?"

She nodded. "Or you may call me Tía Alma if you like; that is what Anita calls me. *Tía* means aunt."

"I hope," said John, "that I will have the right to call you *aunt* . . . someday soon."

"Yes? Ah! I understand. That would please me very much."

"So you call her Anita?"

"Most of the time. Unless we are annoyed with her . . . or if we are being ceremonious . . . then we say 'María Anita.' The other one is more often called María because 'María Concepción' is rather long. Then I also have a great-niece—Guadalupe's granddaughter—María Luisa—who is called by both names all the time. I can see," she finished, "that it would be very confusing to an easterner like you."

"A 'poor, benighted foreigner'," he said. "That's what *she* called me."

Doña Alma laughed.

"Anita called you that? Well, I don't think you will be one for very long."

"No, I hope not," said John. Then he gasped, "My God! I wished her happiness!"

"Who? Anita?"

"Yes! I told her I thought Carson was a fine fellow, and I wished her happiness! Whatever will she think?"

"She will think you were mistaken, as you were," Doña Alma assured him calmly, "and she will realize that you will discover your error, as you have. Don't worry, Mr. Vanderburg, everything will be all right."

"Please call me John," he said.

"John," she repeated, smiling. "I saw how you congratulated Mr. Carson the other morning at the store. I understand now what a very, very fine thing that was! Now, I am going to leave you to compose yourself," she went on, "while I run over to Jorge's house, or I will not have time to fix supper. You will be here for supper, will you not?"

"Yes . . . Yes, I will. You won't give me away, will you, Doña Alma?"

"No one will find out anything from me," she said firmly. "Not even Jim."

CHAPTER TWENTY-ONE

In Las Tunas, Anita spent almost all day Sunday out of doors. She could not bear to be confined in the house, and she had to keep her mother from looking too closely into her face. So she went early out to the garden and worked there all morning, and after lunch she took a long walk.

By Monday morning she had achieved a dry-eyed calm, but she had to keep working to maintain it, so she put on an old dress and prepared to return to the garden.

"I don't know why you are working so hard in that garden," said Doña Guadalupe, "when we will be leaving here soon. I don't imagine Mr. Vanderburg will want to bother with a vegetable garden."

"Probably not," sighed Anita, "but I don't care whether he wants it or not. I am going to see that it is in good shape when he gets it."

She went outside and began to weed the corn patch. Thank God there were plenty of weeds to pull. She had always cursed them before; now she was grateful for them.

Shortly after eleven, Emeterio returned home from his morning's work in town and Anita saw him go into the house. A few moments later Doña Guadalupe came hurrying out to the garden.

"Anita!" she called. "You must come in at once! Mr.

Vanderburg is coming."

"What do you mean? Coming here? When?"

"Now! This afternoon!"

"How do you know?"

"Emeterio saw him. He was checking into the hotel, and he told Emeterio that he was coming up here after lunch."

"What does he want?"

"Oh! I have no idea, but you must come in and clean up. You are a sight!"

"All right, Mamá. I am coming."

She got wearily to her feet and went into the house.

Her mother was hurriedly straightening the parlor while Concha was busy in the kitchen. Anita went on to her room, poured water into the bowl on the washstand, and soaped her face and arms. Her motions were heavy and mechanical; she was filled with a feeling of futility. What was it all for? Why should she go to all this bother for a man who cared nothing for her, even wished to avoid her? Tears prickled in her eyes, but she fought them back angrily. She would not let him see how much she cared! No bother was too much to keep him from knowing that! She would make sure that, in appearance at least, she was cool and polite and unconcerned. And very, very ladylike!

When she joined her mother in the parlor, she was properly gowned and corseted, calm and dignified. She ate a light lunch with the others and afterwards picked up her embroidery and took it out onto the porch. There she ensconced herself in the swing and proceeded to work little flowers and curlicues onto the cloth. She was the perfect picture of a genteel young lady occupied in pleasant pastime.

After a few moments her mother came out to join her, bringing her tatting, and cast an approving glance at Anita. Doña Guadalupe was pleased with her daughter and happy with life for the first time in many months. She had the comfortable feeling that fate was at last behaving as it should, and the effect of that assurance was plain to be seen in her face.

It was quiet in the yard, with only the occasional song of the mockingbird and a slight, fitful breeze in the branches of the pepper trees. Anita heard the trotting of John's horse before he turned into the drive. She kept her eyes modestly on her embroidery until he brought the buggy to a stop in front of the porch; then she rose from the swing and stood quietly behind her mother. He tied the reins and descended from the gig, taking off his hat as he approached.

Doña Guadalupe greeted him cordially. "Good afternoon, Mr. Vanderburg. We did not expect to see you again so soon."

"Good afternoon, Mrs. Aldon—and Miss Aldon. No, I did not expect to be here so soon myself."

"How are Mrs. Vanderburg and your brother? And Miss Collingwood?"

"They have left for the east."

"Already? I understood they had been here only a few days."

"Yes, but my brother had some rather urgent business at home and was unable to stay longer. They left on the train yesterday. That is why I was able to move out to Las Tunas today."

"Do sit down, Mr. Vanderburg. So you are staying at the hotel now?"

"Yes. I intend to remain here at least another month, depending on how things develop. I want to get to know Las Tunas—the town and the country as well as the people."

He turned to Anita, smiling, but she had seated herself again and was earnestly concentrating on her stitches.

"Why, I think that's very nice," commented Doña

Guadalupe. "Would you like some lemonade, Mr. Vanderburg? I believe Concha has some already made."

"No, thank you. As a matter of fact, I thought, since it is such a pleasant afternoon, that Miss Aldon might consent to take a drive with me. I would be grateful if she would show me around the town and perhaps introduce me to some of the residents."

Anita looked up in amazement, and Doña Guadalupe was plainly surprised and pleased.

"Why, how nice! I am sure she would be happy to accompany you, would you not, Anita?"

"I . . . I suppose I could go . . . if you are sure . . . it is what you want . . . ?"

She looked directly into his face and saw that he was gazing steadily at her with an unmistakable warmth.

"I am *very* sure," he said.

"Let me . . . get my parasol," stammered Anita.

"You will not need it," said her mother, "the buggy has a top."

"Oh, so it does."

Struggling to hide her confusion, she laid aside her embroidery, then arose and permitted John to lead her out to the gig and assist her to climb in.

"We will be back in an hour or two, Mrs. Aldon," said John.

"Yes, of course. Have a nice time."

And then the horse was trotting down the drive and into the road, and she was actually riding beside him in the buggy. The seat was narrow, and his arm occasionally brushed hers, and she at once became acutely conscious of his nearness. Her thoughts whirled, and she could make no sense of any of them. She only knew that she was really here, close to him, where she wanted to be; that alone was enough to fill her with warmth and well-being.

"It's a lovely day," he said.

"Yes. Isn't it?"

"Shall we drive up to the old cemetery?"

"The cemetery?"

"I thought it would be a nice ride."

"But . . . I thought you wanted to see the town . . . and meet the people."

"Oh, we can do that any time. I'd rather take a nice long drive first."

Some of her confidence returned and she gave him a sidelong glance.

"After all," she said, looking down modestly, "you did say it would be better if we did not meet alone."

He turned to look at her, and smiled. "Did I say that?"

"Yes."

"Well . . ." he said slowly, turning back to the road, "maybe it *would* be better, but we're going to do it anyway."

She looked at him sharply, but he kept his attention on the horse and said nothing more.

They were both silent as they drove through town, and Anita saw Mrs. Sanders, the dressmaker, step out of the grocery and stare openly as they passed. A moment later they encountered Mr. Lawson in his smart turn-out behind his gray gelding.

"Good afternoon, Lawson," said John.

"Afternoon," replied Lawson, staring at Anita as the vehicles passed.

They left the town behind and drove eastward between the cultivated fields. On the right they approached a little adobe house where Don Alejandro's chief vintner had lived when Anita was a child. The vintner had long since departed, and the house stood empty.

"I wonder if you can advise me, Miss Aldon," said John.

"Advise you?" she asked wonderingly.

"Yes. I think, now that I am a landowner, it would be nice to live on my own property rather than at the hotel. I would like to set up temporary quarters in one of these little adobes while I am building a permanent home. Do you think this one would do?" And he gestured toward the little house on the right.

She looked at the house and then back at John. "You said . . . on your own land."

"This is my land."

"But it is not part of ours . . ."

"No. I bought it from Lawson . . . Do you think that little house would be comfortable for me?"

"I don't know," she murmured. "I don't know what you want."

"Just a temporary home, as I said, while I decide where to build my real home."

"Why, then, I guess this would do, if it were cleaned up and furnished."

He said nothing more as the road wound through the last of the fields and began to climb through the brush of the first low foothills. When they reached the cemetery, he tied the horse and helped Anita down. Then he took her hand under his arm, as she had seen him do with Miss Collingwood, and they strolled in among the grave markers.

"I'm going to have someone clean the weeds out of here," he said.

She drew in a breath sharply. "Is *this* your land, too?" she asked.

"Yes. Is there anything else you'd like me to do here? Fence it in, perhaps?"

"Yes . . ." she said humbly. "Yes. I'd like that."

"I'm thirsty," he said. "Let's walk down to the spring and get a drink."

She couldn't answer him but allowed him to lead her out of the cemetery and down the hill to the canyon below. Climbing down was a little awkward for her because of the unaccustomed corset and the necessity of guarding her good dress from being torn on the branches of the bushes, but it was nice to have John put a helping hand on her arm. Once, when she almost tripped, his arm went quickly around her waist and steadied her. She decided that in some ways it was quite pleasant being a lady.

When they reached the floor of the canyon and started walking toward the big sycamores, John spoke again. "I guess you must have thought I was three kinds of a fool for that silly mistake I made. Doña Alma, bless her heart, finally straightened me out."

"What mistake?" she asked.

"About you and Carson being engaged."

"Mr. Carson engaged to me!"

"Yes. Frankly, I don't remember exactly what I said, but I know I wished you happiness."

She stopped and looked at him in wonderment. "Yes, you did. Was *that* what you meant?"

"Didn't you know?"

"No. I didn't understand it at all." They started walking again. "But why did you think I was engaged to Mr. Carson?"

"Your aunt said he was going to marry her niece, María, and I thought it was you."

"It is my cousin," she said.

"I know that now. Doña Alma explained it all to me last night. She said that *you* are not called María."

"Sometimes I am, but usually I am just Anita."

"You will always be María to me," he said.

They had reached the sycamores and walked slowly under the huge, white branches where the sunlight filtered down in bright splotches on the ground.

"But if you didn't understand me," he went on, "what in the world did you think I meant when I said we shouldn't meet again?"

She looked up into his eyes and said honestly, "I thought it was because I am so different from Mrs. Vanderburg and Miss Collingwood . . . and all your friends."

"But I don't understand. How would that make me not want to see you?"

"Because they are ladies," she went on wistfully. "Such beautiful ladies! And you are a gentleman. They belong to your class, but I . . . I'll never be a real lady. My mother is, but I'm not."

Tears began oozing out onto her lashes, but she couldn't help it.

"María!—Anita—whatever your name is—how can you say a thing like that? You *are* a lady! Oh, my dear, don't you know it is because you *are* different that I love you so?"

Her heart gave a great leap. "Oh, John! Do you love me?"

He took her into his arms and cradled her head against his chest.

"I love you more than anything in the world," he whispered with his lips against her hair. "I've been through hell thinking you were going to marry Carson."

"Even though I am dark and brown and not pink and white . . . like Miss Collingwood?"

"You are not dark and brown! You are golden and glorious! Miss Collingwood is as pale as a sheet. Listen to me, dearest," he went on seriously. "You don't know what you are talking about. Maybe some men like pale women and mincing manners, but I don't. And never forget that real ladies are ladies all the way through, and it doesn't matter what color their skin is, or what they wear. Miss Collingwood doesn't know that and all her pretty gowns can't hide how really vulgar she is; it shows every time she speaks. *You* are a *real* lady, and it shows, whether you're dressed up, or in calico with your beautiful hair down your back." And he pressed his lips into the wavy mass over her forehead.

She was crying openly now.

"I knew that . . . really," she said. "That's why it hurt so to think that *she* had you and I didn't."

"She doesn't have me," he said firmly, "but *you* do . . . if you'll take me."

He pulled away and smiled down at her, his eyes crinkling at the corners the way she remembered them.

"Wait a minute," he said. "I'm getting ahead of myself. I had it all planned out so carefully, but when I touch you, I forget everything."

"Forget what?"

"Come here."

He took her hand and led her to the spot beside the spring where they had eaten their picnic lunch.

"Look," he said. "Let's play house. We'll let this be your *patio,* and that will be the view from your porch over here. Dearest, I'll build you a house here, if you'll let me. This place is yours. I bought it for you. Even if you don't want *me,* this place is still yours . . . but I hope you'll take me with it. Will you marry me and be my wife and play house with me for the rest of our lives?"

She was laughing and wiping her tears at the same time. "Oh, John, yes! I want to be your wife! I have dreamed of it and longed for it!"

He pulled her to him again, and when she lifted her face to

his, she felt the soft, hungry weight of his mouth on hers. Her whole being filled with the fire of his kiss, and she clung to him.

But suddenly she pulled away and stepped back. "Oh!" she cried in frustration, "this isn't the way I wanted it to be!"

"Why, what is the matter?" he asked, in bewilderment. "I tried so hard to make everything perfect. What did I do wrong?"

"Nothing, nothing!" she answered, stamping her foot.

"Then what is wrong?"

"Oh, John! It's just that . . . I have longed so for you to kiss me . . . and hold me . . . but not like this."

"How, then? Tell me."

She looked up into his eyes. "I did so want it to be without this . . . infernal corset!" she whispered, and her face flooded with color.

For an instant he stared, uncomprehending, and then a great, happy laugh shook him, and he folded her tightly in his arms until their bodies swayed together with his laughter.

"Oh, my adorable little darling!" he cried. "I have wanted to hold you, too—without the corset—ever since I first saw you. But never mind, my sweet, barefoot, whistling angel! It won't be long until I hold you without it, and then . . ." He buried his face against her neck and whispered, "I'll even help you take it off!"